"Pl

over

Forr

"Le

out

As

they

hair

Joe

tow

ano

One

wre

to

wer

"

Ju

p

The Hardy Boys
Mystery Stories

Available from MINSTREL Books

124

The HARDY BOYS®

MYSTERY WITH A DANGEROUS BEAT

FRANKLIN W. DIXON

A MINSTREL® BOOK

PUBLISHED BY POCKET BOOKS

New York   London   Toronto   Sydney   Tokyo   Singapore

A MINSTREL PAPERBACK *ORIGINAL*

 A Minstrel Book published by
POCKET BOOKS, a division of Simon & Schuster Inc.
1230 Avenue of the Americas, New York, NY 10020

Copyright © 1994 by Simon & Schuster Inc.
Front cover illustration by Brian Kotzky

Produced by Mega-Books of New York, Inc.

All rights reserved, including the right to reproduce
this book or portions thereof in any form whatsoever.
For information address Pocket Books, 1230 Avenue
of the Americas, New York, NY 10020

ISBN: 0-671-79314-4

First Minstrel Books printing February 1994

10 9 8 7 6 5 4 3 2

THE HARDY BOYS MYSTERY STORIES is a trademark
of Simon & Schuster Inc.

THE HARDY BOYS, A MINSTREL BOOK, and colophon
are registered trademarks of Simon & Schuster Inc.

Printed in the U.S.A.

Contents

MYSTERY WITH A DANGEROUS BEAT

1 Mobbed!

"We want the Funky Four!" the crowd around Joe Hardy chanted loudly. "We want the Funky Four!"

The house lights faded to black at the huge Los Angeles Century Auditorium. Fans leapt to their feet, shouting for the group as the brilliant stage lights came on. Joe and his brother, Frank, sitting in the fourth row of the arena, joined in the shouting and clapping.

"We want the Funky Four!" Joe shouted. "Encore! Funky Four!"

Joe couldn't believe his luck. He and his older brother Frank, who was eighteen, had gotten floor seats to one of the hottest concerts of the year. The Funky Four had already played a two-hour set, and the crowd wasn't about to let them go.

Next to Joe, Frank shook his head in amazement. "I knew the Funky Four were popular," Frank yelled over the roar of the crowd, "but this is unreal!"

"The band's last album went multiplatinum," Joe shouted back. "Every single show on their tour has been sold out."

It was the middle of February, and the Hardys had flown to California five days ago with their mother, father, and Aunt Gertrude. Earlier in the day they had gone on the Universal Studios tour along with Harold Manstroni, a friend of their parents. Manstroni was employed by musicians as a personal manager.

"I can't believe Mr. Manstroni just offered us these tickets," Joe said. The crowd was getting even louder, and the floor had started vibrating with their pounding feet. "This is the best show I've ever been to, and I didn't even have to wait in a ticket line for hours!"

"The Funky Four are even better live than they are on CD," Frank said, running a hand through his thick brown hair and straining to see above the crowd.

"You can say that again," Joe replied. "These guys have got to be the best dance band around."

Seventeen-year-old Joe watched the colored stage lights stream across the auditorium. Lasers and strobes added to all the excitement as the crowd grew even wilder. Finally, a heavy synthesized drumbeat started to boom over the sound system. Spotlights flashed across the crowd, then settled on the stage, revealing the return of the Funky Four's impressive backup band—two guitarists, a bass player, a keyboard player, a drummer, and a deejay surrounded by turntables and samplers.

The band started into their encore. Suddenly, a loud roar came from the back of the huge auditorium. Everyone turned around to see the lead singer and heartthrob, Brian Beat—along with Jason McDermott, J.T. Eckert, and Terry Solinsky— zooming up the aisles on motorcycles! They drove up ramps onto the stage, leapt off their bikes, and began to dance.

All four were dressed alike in black leather jackets, white T-shirts and black bike shorts. Their hair was slicked back and their dance moves were perfectly timed to each other and the music. The lead singer, Brian Beat, grabbed the microphone and started to sing the group's latest number one hit.

"Awesome!" Joe cried, jumping up from his seat while the crowd roared around them.

Of the two Hardys, Joe was the biggest Funky Four fan in the family. Frank liked them, too, and climbed up on his seat for a better look.

"Brian Beat has total star quality," Joe cried out, his blond hair falling into his face. "Look at him!"

Brian came up to the edge of the stage and leaned

3

in to the crowd. The girls in the front row screamed, and the guys reached out to grab his hand.

Joe grinned at Frank and gave the thumbs-up sign as the band went into their second number. The Funky Four performed a series of tumbles that ended in them all doing splits. Then, as the rest of the group continued dancing, Brian stepped to the front of the stage and grabbed the mike. Just as he opened his mouth to sing, a large object plummeted out of the curtains above him. It was a huge spotlight, and it was about to fall on Brian's head!

The crowd let out a gasp. "Watch out!" Joe shouted instinctively.

Brian instantly noticed the crowd's shocked reaction. He looked up, then immediately jumped back, lost his balance, and fell to the floor. The spotlight hit the stage and crashed to pieces, missing him by inches. The bulb shattered, sending glass flying all over the stage.

Next to Joe, a young girl put a hand over her mouth to hold back a cry. Several fans jostled the Hardys as they pushed by to get closer to the stage to see if Brian was all right. Two members of the Funky Four went rushing over to the star, who was still on his back, propped up on his elbows and looking dazed. Someone from the road crew ran out from behind the stage and knelt beside Brian. They were all joined by a middle-aged man with graying hair and a two-day growth of beard. The men conferred for a moment, then helped Brian to his feet and led him limping offstage.

The crowd started to grow restless, and Joe watched as finally the man with the graying hair returned and stepped up to the microphone. "Ladies and gentleman, Brian is going to be all right. . . ." he said. The audience let out a cheer. "Unfortunately, due to this unforeseen accident, the concert is now over. Brian got some shards of glass in his leg and needs to be seen by a doctor."

The man was interrupted by Funky Four member Jason McDermott, who tapped him on the shoulder and whispered in his ear. The man shook his head. "Jason tells me that he and the boys are willing to finish the encore without Brian," he said. "But that wouldn't be fair. After all, what are the Funky Four without Brian Beat?"

The crowd screamed in agreement. With that, the band left the stage, along with the other members of the Funky Four. All around Frank and Joe, fans expressed their shock and concern.

As the audience filed out of the auditorium, Joe saw Frank gazing thoughtfully up at the stage.

"If you're thinking what I'm thinking," Joe said, "you're wondering how often one of those spotlights falls by accident?"

"It seems pretty unlikely," Frank replied.

"Let's check it out," Joe said eagerly.

Frank and Joe bucked the flow of the crowd. It wasn't an easy job, but finally they made their way

5

to the edge of the stage. The road crew was dismantling drums and unplugging amplifiers. The smashed spotlight still lay on the floor where it had fallen. The light was about two feet in diameter and looked heavy.

"That could have really hurt Brian," Frank said, pointing out the large light.

"And the shards of glass could have hurt someone in the audience." Joe stepped up to the edge of the stage, which came to his chest, and peered up toward the ceiling, searching for the location where the spotlight had once hung.

"Hey, you two, the concert's over," a burly security guard with a stringy ponytail said, stepping up beside them.

"We're just looking around," Frank said. "Do you know how those spotlights are held in place?"

"Who wants to know?" the man growled.

"I'm Joe Hardy and this is my brother, Frank," Joe began.

"Look, I don't care who you are. You're not going backstage, and that's final."

"We don't want to go backstage," Frank said. "We just want—"

"To meet the Funky Four," the security man said. "Yeah, yeah. So does everyone else in North America. But it isn't gonna happen. Now get out of here—or do I have to carry you out?"

Frank and Joe looked at each other. "I think this

is one mystery that's going to have to remain unsolved," Frank said. "At least for the time being."

"Oh, no! Here comes a Mack truck!" Joe cried, frantically pressing the buttons on the Hack Attack video game machine. On the screen, a speeding truck barreled into Joe's taxi, crushing it flat. The machine emitted a loud crash, and the words GAME OVER appeared on screen.

"Better luck next time," Frank said without taking his eyes off the Air Racer game he was playing.

It was the morning after the Funky Four concert, and Frank and Joe were in a video arcade at Venice Beach. Frank and Joe's Aunt Gertrude had insisted on taking a bus tour through Beverly Hills to view the homes of the stars. Mr. and Mrs. Hardy had agreed to go along, but Frank and Joe had opted to spend the morning hanging out at the beach.

It was a sunny Saturday, and Venice Beach was packed with people. Outside the arcade, girls flew by on Rollerblades and a group of kids was headed to a ramp with their skateboards. Along the boardwalk, psychics promised to predict the future for two dollars. Even though it was only February, the weather was warm and sunny and the beach was packed with sunbathers. Some surfers were even riding the waves off in the distance. As they had been driving to the beach from their hotel in

Hollywood, Frank and Joe could see the mountains off in the distance, and some of them actually had snow on their peaks.

As Joe slipped another coin into the Hack Attack machine, a young man in a baseball cap, gray sweats, and mirrored sunglasses walked into the arcade. He had a thick, dark mustache and walked with a slight limp.

Frank kept playing his video game, but Joe turned to look at the young guy. Despite his limp, the man moved with agility. Joe turned away, then looked again. There was something about the guy that seemed strangely familiar.

The young man stepped up to the machine next to Joe and reached into his pocket for money. "Oh man," he muttered. "I can't believe it!"

"What's wrong?" Joe asked.

"I left my wallet at home." He laughed self-consciously. "I'm not used to carrying money anymore. I mean," he added quickly, "everybody uses credit cards these days, you know?"

Frank glanced away from his game and looked over at Joe. "I've got another two games on this machine," Frank said. "You want to go one on one?"

"You bet!"

The young man joined Frank at the Air Racer machine. When Joe's game ended, he went over to watch them. He took a close look at the stranger's

8

high cheekbones and sandy hair. The mustache was definitely a fake. But the limp was for real. Suddenly something clicked.

"Brian Beat!" he cried.

The young man glanced around nervously, obviously checking to see if anyone else in the arcade had heard his name. But the other players hardly looked up from their games.

"Yeah, you got me," Brian said at last, lifting his sunglasses to reveal his famous green eyes. "Just don't tell anyone else, okay? I'm trying to spend the day being a normal person. As if that's possible!"

"I can't believe it! Brian Beat, in person," Joe said. "We were at your show last night. It was incredible!"

Frank glanced down at Brian's leg. "Are you doing okay? We saw the accident."

"No problema. I could have finished the show, but Marcus, our manager, insisted I see a doctor. Can't let his precious property get damaged," he added sarcastically.

"Has that kind of accident happened before?" Frank asked.

Brian shook his head. "Lucky for me and the band, no."

"Did the technicians figure out what happened?" Joe asked.

"Nope," Brian said. "But if I know Marcus, somebody got fired over it. Everyone's feeling pretty stressed. We're finishing up a six-month tour, and every night we don't have a gig we're in the studio recording our new album. Now we're about to shoot the first video and then start promoting the single." He glanced away from the game and sighed. Almost instantly, his plane was blasted out of the sky. He laughed. "I think I need a vacation."

The boys fell silent as Frank and Brian concentrated on the video game. Brian grinned happily as he manipulated the joystick to send his fighter plane swooping over an imaginary city.

When the game ended, Brian turned to Frank and Joe. "You guys know me, but I don't know you."

"I'm Frank Hardy and this is my brother, Joe," Frank said. "We're visiting from Bayport, New York."

Brian shook their hands. "Glad to meet you."

"How about another game?" Frank asked.

Brian checked his watch. He was about to answer when suddenly a man in a hooded sweatshirt and dark glasses turned from a nearby machine and ran past them with his head lowered. As he passed Brian, he reached out and pulled off the rock star's fake mustache. Startled, Brian jerked his head back, and the sudden action knocked off his hat and sunglasses.

"Brian Beat!" the stranger shouted as he streaked out the doorway and disappeared.

"Brian Beat?" the man at the change booth repeated. He looked at Brian. "Hey, it is! Brian Beat is in my arcade!"

With a look of panic in his eyes, Brian ran for the entrance. But it was too late. As soon as he stepped outside, he was surrounded by dozens of screaming fans.

"Please, you'll all get autographs," Brian shouted over the screams of the crowd. "Just form a line! Form a line!" But the excited fans just pressed in closer.

"Come on," Joe said to Frank. "If we don't get him out of there, he'll be crushed."

Joe ran to the arcade entrance, with Frank close behind. Together they began pushing through the crowd that had formed at the doorway. As they moved, they kept their eyes on Brian's sandy hair in the middle of the mob. But before Frank and Joe could get close to him, they saw two beefy guys push toward Brian. The two guys collided with one another, and one of them raised a fist to hit the other.

Brian tried to step between the two young men. "Please, stop," he said.

But Brian was too late. One guy shoved the other, and the two began a wrestling match. The crowd began to overreact. People began pushing each other to avoid being stomped on, and several screams were heard over the noise of the mob. Then

11

the owner of the arcade called out for someone to get the police.

"We've got to stop this before it turns into a riot!" Joe cried.

"Come on!" Frank yelled.

Just then, Joe saw Brian fall backward and disappear beneath the feet of the unruly mob.

2 A Crazy Stunt

Frank and Joe frantically pushed through the crowd. But their progress was slow. Excited fans elbowed them, stepped on their feet, and shoved them aside in an effort to get closer to Brian.

The two guys who had started the fight were going at it full blast, punching and kicking each other. Brian was nowhere in sight, and the screaming fans kept calling out his name.

"He's getting trampled!" Frank cried out.

Somehow Frank had to break up the crowd, and there was only one way he could think of to do it. "Fire!" he shouted at the top of his lungs. "Fire!"

Joe looked at him in surprise, then understood. "Fire!" he yelled. "Run for your life!"

The fans in front of Frank and Joe hesitated. A few of them turned and ran toward the beach. That was the opening the Hardys needed. They shoved their way through the crowd until they saw Brian. He was curled up on the ground, trying to fend off the stomping feet and groping hands.

Joe got to him first. He grabbed Brian's arm and helped him to his feet. Frank acted as defensive lineman, clearing the way with his muscular arms and shoulders while Joe dragged Brian out of the crowd and into a nearby ice cream store. With Frank right behind them, they ran through the store and out the back door into an alleyway.

"My car's at the next intersection," Brian said breathlessly, pointing down the alley. "Come on!"

Frank, Joe, and Brian took off down the alley. Finally, they reached the corner. There was a parking lot to the right. Brian ran down the rows until he came to a black Porsche convertible. Suddenly, the locks on the doors opened with a click.

"Magic," Brian said, holding out a remote with his keys attached to it. He leaped into the car and tossed the keys to Frank. "You drive!" Brian shouted. "I'll hide in the back, just in case they're still following us."

Frank jumped into the driver's seat, and Joe hopped into the passenger's seat. Brian wedged himself into the tiny space behind the seats. With a squeal of rubber, Frank tore out of the parking lot.

At that moment, a pack of running fans appeared from the alley.

"Phew!" Brian said as they pulled away. "That was too real."

"Are you all right?" Frank asked, glancing at Brian. His clothes were torn and his hair was tousled.

"Just a few scrapes," he replied. "Turn here," he said, catching his breath. "I seem to be having really bad luck lately."

"If you ask me, that guy in the video arcade was no fan," Frank said. "He deliberately revealed your identity so you'd be mobbed."

"It sounds to me as if someone's out to get you," Joe said. "But why?"

"I have no idea," Brian answered. "But I'd sure like to find out."

"Maybe we can help," Frank suggested. "We've investigated lots of crimes."

"You have?" Brian asked, surprised.

"You bet," said Frank, and explained that the Hardys' father, a renowned private investigator, had taught them the business of fighting crime.

While Brian gave Frank directions, Joe said, "I've got an idea. If you can get us hired on the video shoot as extras or something, we can keep an eye on you and do some investigating at the same time."

Frank saw Brian's face light up. "That sounds perfect," Brian said as Frank pulled onto the free-

15

way. "We can talk to Marcus, the band's manager, about it today. But I don't see any problem with you guys being extras."

"Great," Frank said. "Just make sure you don't tell anyone we're detectives. We can do a better job if we work anonymously."

"No problem," Brian answered. "I'll just tell everyone you're friends of mine from the video arcade."

Fifteen minutes later, Brian and the Hardys were driving through downtown Los Angeles. Brian let Frank use the car phone to leave a message at the hotel for their parents that they wouldn't be back until later.

"Aunt Gertrude sure will be shocked," Joe said with a smile, "when she finds out we're helping you out, Brian."

"Not to mention the kids back home," Frank added.

"And appearing in a video," Brian said, laughing. "Maybe it'll be the start of a big career."

Frank pulled up at the back of an elegant old theater. The sign above the stage door said The Rialto.

"The video we're making is for our new single, 'Can't Catch Me,'" Brian explained. "In it the Funky Four play spies being chased by a female villain and her henchmen."

"That sounds cool," Joe said.

"Today we're shooting the band while we lip-synch the song on stage," Brian answered. "We'll intercut that with the action shots in the final edit."

As the Hardys and Brian climbed out, the backstage door burst open and Marcus Malone appeared. "Well, it's about time!" the manager said angrily. He held up a copy of the music magazine *Dance Party Scene*. "What's the meaning of this?"

"The meaning of what?" Brian asked blankly.

Marcus stopped dead and stared at Brian. He took in the star's ripped clothes and scraped face and demanded, "What happened to you?"

"I was recognized in a video arcade at Venice Beach," he said. He turned to Frank and Joe. "These guys helped me escape. This is Frank Hardy and his brother, Joe."

Marcus barely glanced at them. "You idiot!" he growled. "What in the world were you doing at Venice Beach?"

"Gimme a break, will you?" Brian muttered. "I just need to hang like a normal guy once in a while."

Marcus rolled his eyes and said, "But you're not a normal guy, Brian, and I think it's about time you realized that. If you want to play video games, we'll have some installed in your house."

Frank felt uncomfortable watching Marcus talk to Brian like this. He glanced at Joe, who was pretending to look off into the distance. He could tell Joe

17

didn't like what he heard, either. But Marcus didn't seem to mind having this conversation in front of them, and Frank wasn't about to take a walk just so the guy could yell at Brian.

"It's not the same," Brian protested. "Sometimes I just want to be with real people."

"What about the other guys in the band?"

Brian sighed. "Jason, J.T., and Terry are my best friends, but they're in the business just like me. Besides, we never have time to hang out together anymore. We're too busy rehearsing with the band, learning new dance steps, recording, touring. I need a break sometimes, you know?"

Marcus put his hands on his hips. "Is that why you told *Dance Party Scene* you're quitting the group?"

"What?" Brian asked uncertainly. "What are you talking about?"

"It's right here in Pico Hernandez's gossip column." Marcus opened the magazine and began to read out loud. "'The contract between manager Marcus Malone and his superstar discovery the Funky Four expires at the end of this month. Jason, J.T., and Terry say they plan to re-sign with Malone, but what about lead singer Brian Beat? Could it be he's looking for greener pastures? Stay tuned for further developments.'"

"Oh, lighten up, Marcus," Brian said with a laugh. "You know Pico Hernandez will do anything to sell magazines. He asked me if I was going to sign a new contract with you, and I said it was none of his business. Now he's trying to turn it into a big deal."

"Well, why didn't you just tell him yes?" Marcus asked irritably.

Brian scowled. "Because I don't like him. Why should I tell him anything? He doesn't care about the music and he doesn't care about me. All that matters to him is uncovering the dirt."

"That's his job," Marcus said heatedly. "And your job is to be nice to him. *Dance Party Scene* is a very influential magazine. Pico's inside right now, along with a lot of other reporters. They're all asking questions about this story. I want you to go tell him you're going to sign a new contract with me. And while you're at it, plug the group's new single."

Frank saw Brian sigh. "All right," Brian said wearily. He seemed too tired to fight anymore. "Listen, Marcus," he added, "can you do me a favor? Frank and Joe helped me out of a tight spot. I want to return the favor by letting them be extras in the video."

"Sure, sure," Marcus said with a wave of his hand, barely glancing at Frank and Joe. "Just promise me you won't go wandering around in public places anymore. A little publicity is fine, but I don't want my hottest property ripped limb from limb by

19

a mob of crazed teenyboppers. Now, come on. We've got a lot of work to do today." He put his arm around Brian's shoulders and led him inside.

Frank and Joe followed. They found themselves backstage in a hallway lined with dressing rooms. Dozens of people were rushing up and down the hall. A woman came by pushing a wardrobe rack filled with clothing. A pizza delivery boy came the other way carrying a stack of pizzas. Stagehands carried lights, video monitors, and amplifiers.

"We need you in wardrobe, then makeup," Marcus told Brian. "Then I've got you scheduled for five minutes with Pico and some of the other reporters. Afterward, we'll do a quick run-through of the new dance steps, rehearse with the band a few times, and shoot the scene." He patted Brian on the back. "Piece of cake."

"Sure," Brian replied. "Just give me ten minutes to take a quick shower. Where's my dressing room?"

"Right down there," he said, pointing to a door with a silver star on it. "And hurry. This shoot is costing major bucks, and we've got three more days to go."

"What about us?" Frank asked.

"Report to Mindy Beckett," Brian said. "She's the second A.D.—assistant director, that is. She's in charge of all the extras."

"Where do we find her?" Joe asked.

"Ask someone on the crew," Marcus said brusquely. With that, Marcus turned his back on Frank and Joe and ushered Brian into his dressing room.

"Nice guy," Frank said sarcastically, watching Marcus disappear.

"Yeah, if you like lizards," Joe replied.

Frank felt for Brian. Now he could see why the guy just wanted to hang out in a video arcade like any kid.

"Marcus acts as if the Funky Four would be nowhere without him," Frank said scornfully.

"He may be right," Joe said. "I read that he discovered the group two years ago when they were singing in a shopping mall. They were just out of high school. Marcus has guided their career every step of the way."

"And I'll bet he never lets them forget it, either," Frank said. He noticed a woman with a comb and a bottle of hair spray hurrying toward them. "Excuse me," he said. "We're extras. Do you know where we can find Mindy Beckett?"

"Extras are supposed to enter through the front door," she snapped. "Backstage is off-limits except to the band and the crew."

"Sorry," Joe said. "We're friends of Brian Beat. We came in with him."

The woman's already cool expression turned frosty. "Oh, I see. Now he's not only firing people,

21

he's hiring them, too." She frowned. "Go down this hall and turn right. Mindy is the tall one with the red hair."

"What was that all about?" Frank asked as the woman walked on.

"Beats me," Joe replied. "It sounds as if Brian fired someone and she's not too happy about it."

"Well, let's find Mindy," Frank said.

Joe nodded. "And while we're at it, we can try to figure out if anyone else is mad at Brian—and why. It's almost too easy with all this excitement to forget we're on a case!"

Frank laughed as he and Joe walked back down the hall in the direction of the door that led to the stage. On the wall, an arrow-shaped sign with the words To the Stage pointed to the right. They were just about to turn the corner when the growl of a revving engine split the air.

"You hear that?" Frank asked, looking back at Joe.

Joe nodded. "I sure do. Maybe it's some kind of equipment for the video shoot."

An instant later, the door from the street behind them burst open and a man on a red Harley-Davidson roared through it—heading right for them!

3 Zapped

"Watch out!" Frank cried, grabbing Joe's shirt-sleeve.

Joe's heart pounded as he and Frank leapt back and pressed themselves against the wall. A young woman carrying a microphone stand jumped in the other direction.

The motorcycle screeched to a halt, just two feet in front of Joe and Frank. The roar of the engine bounced off the walls and created a deafening noise until the driver turned it off. Then he removed his helmet. He ran his hand through his spiky brown hair, unzipped his expensive black leather jacket, and smiled. "Hi, everybody! Am I late?"

"You moron!" Joe cried, his breath ragged. "You could have killed someone!"

The young man scowled and his dark eyes flashed angrily. "Don't you know who I am?"

As soon as the guy spoke, Joe recognized him immediately. But he was still too steamed up to be starstruck. "Sure," Joe replied. "You're Jason McDermott of the Funky Four. Big deal. I don't care if you're the president of the United States. That was a dangerous stunt you just pulled."

Joe saw Brian's dressing room door open down the hall. "What's all the commotion?" he asked. Then he saw Jason. "Hey, Jas, what's up?"

Frank was just about to answer when Jason spoke up. "I'm just about to pound this twerp," Jason said. "You want to help me?"

Joe and Frank exchanged a look. "What a turkey," Joe said under his breath.

Brian left his dressing room and walked down the hall. "Hey, lighten up. These guys are my friends. They saved me from a screaming mob at the video arcade. Jason, meet Frank and Joe Hardy."

Jason looked the Hardys up and down. Then he smiled. "Well, any friend of Brian is a friend of mine. I'm sorry if I scared you," he added, holding out his hand. "I was just fooling around."

Joe and Frank shook Jason's hand. "And I'm sorry I lost my temper," Joe said, a little reluctantly.

"Hey, what happened to you, man?" Brian asked Jason. "You were supposed to meet me at Venice Beach two hours ago."

"Sorry. I got caught in a traffic jam on the San Diego Freeway."

"Well, you better get changed. We have to talk to some reporters before the shoot. There's a rumor going around that I'm not going to sign a new contract with Marcus next month."

"You aren't?" Jason asked quickly.

"Sure I am. I mean, that's what everyone wants, right?"

"Well, sure," Jason said. "What would the Funky Four be without Brian Beat?"

Brian laughed. "That's what Marcus said." He put his arm around Jason's shoulders. "Come on, man. Let's get to work."

While Brian and Jason headed back to their dressing rooms, Frank and Joe made their way to the stage. They found themselves in a beautiful old theater with gold cherubs on the walls and crystal chandeliers hanging from the ceiling. The theater was alive with activity. The crew members were setting up instruments, moving lights, and looking through video cameras. All the seats to the theater were packed with people, and a woman was speaking to them.

"That must be Mindy Beckett," Frank said. They walked back to meet her. "Excuse me, are we in the right place? We're extras."

The tall woman with curly red hair and flashing blue eyes sized them up. "You're in the right place

25

all right. With those great muscles you could be stuntmen. Do you have any experience?"

"Not exactly, but we're pretty athletic," Joe said, a little embarrassed at Mindy's comment. "We surf and skateboard."

"Can you ride a Jet Ski?"

"Sure," Frank said.

"Good. Today we're shooting audience reactions. You can be in the crowd. Tomorrow we'll use you in the Jet Ski scene." She turned to the crowd. "Please sit quietly, everyone. The makeup and wardrobe folks will look you over, and please be sure to fill in all the seats in the front rows."

Frank and Joe took seats in the audience. Finally, a husky, bearded man in a black baseball cap stepped from behind a camera and spoke to the crowd.

"I'm the director, Lenny Wiseman," he said. "Here's what we have planned today. The Funky Four are going to come out and do a short interview with the press. Then they'll run through their dance steps. After that, we shoot the scenes. Your job is to scream and jump around when the group performs, and keep quiet the rest of the time. Any questions?" He didn't wait for an answer. "Okay, good. Here come the boys now."

The Hardys watched as the Funky Four walked out and sat on the edge of the stage. They were all dressed alike in brightly colored baggies, white T-shirts, and black denim jackets. Joe realized that

Brian was definitely the best looking of the four, with his sandy hair and piercing green eyes. Beside Brian sat Jason. He had spiky brown hair and dark eyes that constantly searched the room. J.T. Eckert was next. He was shorter than the others, with blond hair and a boyish face. Beside him was Terry Solinsky. He was tall and lanky, with a wide, friendly grin.

A side door opened and Marcus Malone led ten reporters and several photographers into the room. They huddled in front of the Funky Four. The photographers started snapping pictures, and the reporters began asking questions about the new album, the tour, and the video.

Even though they were several rows back in the audience, Joe was able to hear most of the reporters' questions, since they were shouted out.

"Is it true you guys wrote some of the songs on the new album?" a reporter asked, her tape recorder held high to get the answer.

"Marcus writes all our songs," Jason piped up. "We had three Top Ten hits off the last album, so why mess with success?"

"What about lead vocals on the new album?" another shouted. "Any changes?"

"Brian's our lead singer," Jason said. "We all have pretty good voices, but we think it's important to have a consistent sound."

"Brian, I know that each of you has a separate contract with Marcus Malone," said a thin man with black hair combed straight back off his face. "What will happen to the rest of the group if you decide to sign with a new manager next month?"

The crowd of reporters started buzzing, and several flashes went off as the photographers captured Brian's expression.

Brian looked up from his hands and frowned. "Look, Pico," he said, "I never said I was signing with a new manager, and you know it. Why do you write that trash?"

Pico ignored the question. "So all of you do plan to re-sign with Marcus next month?" he asked.

"You bet," Terry said.

"Of course," J.T. added.

Jason nodded. "I'm sticking with Marcus. How about you, Brian?"

"Sure," he said with a shrug.

"Brian doesn't look very happy with his decision," Joe whispered to Frank.

"I was just thinking the same thing."

"What if Marcus knows Brian doesn't really want to sign up with him," Joe suggested. "Could he have made that stage light fall on Brian, to scare him?"

"Could be," Frank agreed. "We'll have to keep an eye on Marcus. It seems like the guy's got enough ambition to threaten Brian if he thought he had to."

Marcus stepped to the front of the stage from where he'd been standing. "Okay, that's it, guys," he said. "We've got a video to shoot." He led the reporters and photographers out as the Funky Four took their places on stage.

Around them, the audience grew restless. Joe sensed the extras couldn't wait to start acting like crazed fans.

"Linc, you want to lead the boys through the new steps?" Lenny Wiseman asked.

A man with a sleek dancer's body stepped out of the wings. "All right, fellows, just like we learned yesterday. One, two, three—"

The Funky Four danced while Linc kept the beat by snapping his fingers. They ran through the steps three times with Linc giving them pointers as they moved. On the last run-through, Jason added an extra spin and a clever double-time step.

"Hey, that's good!" Linc exclaimed. "Let's use it."

"Give the step to Brian," Lenny said. "I can come in for a close-up."

"But Jason thought it up," Brian protested.

"I know, and it's terrific," Lenny said. "But I think it'll work better if you step forward and do it."

"That's cool," Jason said. "Go for it, Brian."

The group walked through the steps one more time with Brian adding the extra moves.

"Perfect," Lenny said. "Let's shoot it. Places, everyone. Let's get this scene in the can."

Brian took his place beside Jason, J.T., and Terry. All around Joe and Frank, hundreds of extras rose to their feet and prepared to act like excited fans.

"Wow! This is going to be wild!" Joe exclaimed.

"Awesome," Frank agreed.

"Can't Catch Me, take one," the assistant director announced. "Camera?"

"Rolling," the head cameraman said. He stood behind the huge camera that was attached to a moving crane.

"Roll sound," the assistant director called.

"Action!" Lenny shouted from behind the cameraman.

The opening bars of "Can't Catch Me" blasted through the monitors at the edge of the stage. The Funky Four began to dance. Two video cameras filmed their moves while a third filmed the extras. Frank and Joe jumped up and down with the crowd, screaming like crazed fans and waving their arms in the air.

Brian did his extra spin and double-time step, then stepped forward and reached for the microphone, ready to lip-synch the first line of the song. But as he grabbed the microphone, sparks flew out of it.

Joe watched in horror as Brian's face contorted with pain. With a gasp, Brian fell to the ground with the mike still held tightly in his clenched fist.

"He's being electrocuted!" Joe cried out.

30

4 Trouble on Wheels

Frank struggled past the people in his row to get to the aisle. "Come on!" he called out to Joe. "We've got to help him."

Onstage, Brian was still lying in a heap on the floor, the mike stand beside him. Marcus raced to him from the wings and cried out, "Do something! Somebody!"

Frank rushed to the front of the chest-high stage, with Joe by his side. "Nobody touch him!" Frank shouted. He noticed a makeup woman standing off to the side, holding a towel. Quickly, he grabbed it out of her hands, jumped up onto the stage, and tossed the towel around the microphone stand. Brian lay on the ground, silent and unmoving. Being careful not to touch him, Frank grabbed both ends of the towel and pulled hard. The mike was wrenched out of Brian's hand, breaking the current.

Several people in the crowd let out a gasp as the microphone went flying across the stage. Joe had jumped on the stage right behind Frank. He stepped in and used the towel to pull the plug from the dangerous microphone. Then he knelt down to examine it.

While Joe checked out the microphone, Frank knelt beside Brian. Marcus, Jason, J.T., and Terry also gathered around.

"Hey, buddy, are you all right?" Jason asked.

Frank waited for Brian's eyes to flutter to life, but there was no answer. "Call an ambulance!" Frank urged Marcus.

"Someone dial nine one one!" Marcus hollered into the wings.

But at that moment, Brian's mouth started moving, and his eyes blinked open. "What happened?" he asked weakly.

"You were almost electrocuted," Marcus said.

"Frank saved you by pulling the mike out of your hand," Jason added.

"Twice in one day," Brian said, smiling wanly at Frank. "I really owe you, man."

"Take it easy," Frank urged.

The director and his assistant were trying to keep the crowd quiet, as was the choreographer. Meanwhile, Frank noticed Pico Hernandez standing in the wings, snapping photographs of Brian. Frank wondered how Pico managed to get back in after Marcus had made sure that all the reporters and photographers left the building. Pico sure was sneaky.

"I don't need a doctor," Brian said, getting slowly to his feet. "I'm fine."

Frank offered Brian a hand up. "Be careful. And I'd say you do need a doctor."

"We need to know for sure," Marcus replied anxiously. "I wouldn't want you working if it's dangerous. Even if we have to postpone the video." A grim expression set into his face and he rubbed at his chin.

"Don't worry, Marcus," Brian said sarcastically. "I won't mess up your schedule."

"What concerns me is how something like this could happen," Frank broke in. "If you were only lip-synching the song, why was the mike on in the first place?"

"It wasn't supposed to be," Lenny Wiseman said. "And even if it was turned on accidentally, it shouldn't have caused a shock."

"Here's the answer," Joe said. Everyone turned to look at him. "Someone ran a wire down each side of the mike," he explained, "one with a positive charge and one with a negative charge. When Brian reached for the mike, he completed the circuit and the electricity shot through him."

Frank went over to where Joe was standing. He

quickly saw what Joe meant. "The person who did it disguised the wires by wrapping them in silver tape and running them along the metal ridges on either side of the microphone," he observed.

"So you're saying someone did this on purpose?" J.T. asked incredulously.

Brian's mouth dropped open. Marcus turned to stare into the back of the darkened theater, where the sound crew's mixing board was set up. "Sound crew, get up here! I want an explanation for this and I want it now!"

A man and a woman left the mixing board and hurried up the aisle. Marcus stood on the stage chewing them out. The director finally turned to the audience and said, "Take five, people. Or maybe ten." He ran his hands through his hair in frustration, and Frank could hear him say, "Who knows when we'll get back to work."

J.T., Jason, and Terry all helped Brian into the wings. Some of the extras were leaving the theater when Frank heard a woman's voice in the darkness call out, "There he is! There's the creep who stole my song!"

Brian suddenly turned around. Frank saw an eager look pass over Pico's face, as if he couldn't believe his luck.

A woman dressed in black bike shorts and an oversize denim jacket came Rollerblading up the aisle. Under the jacket she wore an orange top, and part of her brown hair was dyed green.

34

As soon as she appeared, Linc, the choreographer, raised his hands in the air and said, "Oh no. Suzi B.!"

"Suzi B.!" Marcus shouted at her. "I thought we told you this theater was off-limits and that you'd better stay away."

"Where are the reporters?" Suzi wanted to know. She stood in the aisle, her hands on her hips. "I want my own press conference so I can tell the world about how Brian Beat and Marcus Malone are thieves!"

Brian had joined Frank and Joe, with the rest of the Funky Four in tow. Frank turned to him and said, "What's going on, Brian?"

Brian's eyes never left Suzi, who was staring him down. "Suzi B. used to be our choreographer. Then we let her go because of creative differences," he explained.

"Because you didn't want me to know about how you stole my material," Suzi insisted.

Linc tried to intercept Suzi, but the woman skated closer to the stage and spoke to Marcus. "Three months ago I gave Brian a cassette tape of songs I'd just written," she said. "I just heard the Funky Four's new song 'Can't Catch Me.' Guess what? There's absolutely no difference between the songs. And I just happened to be fired right before the band went into the studio to record it, so what do you have to say about that, Mr. Marcus Malone?"

"What are you talking about?" Brian asked,

before Marcus could say anything. "That cassette is still at my house, on the shelf next to the stereo where I left it."

Suzi sneered. "Like I believe that!"

Frank saw Pico Hernandez edge out of the wings. He had a reporter's pad in his hand, and he was taking it all down.

Frank rushed toward him and said, "This is all confidential, bud."

Pico gave Frank a smug grin and replied, "Just doing my job, man. Who are you, the hall monitor?"

When Frank went back to where Joe was, Marcus was standing at the edge of the stage now, holding out his hands in frustration. "Suzi. Try to be reasonable. We did not steal your song."

"Then how do you explain the fact that the chorus of 'Can't Catch Me' sounds suspiciously like the chorus of the first song on my tape?" she asked. "The lyrics are different and the tempo is changed, but it's still my song. I'd know that hook anywhere."

Marcus and Brian exchanged a bewildered look.

"I have no idea," Brian insisted. "But I swear I never gave Marcus your tape!"

Jason tried to step between Brian and Suzi. "Suzi," he said soothingly. "Listen to me. 'Can't Catch Me' is an old song of mine. I wrote it before we even met Marcus. I played him an old demo and we worked on it together."

"If it's your song," Suzi sneered, "why does it sound so much like my song?"

Jason frowned. "It's a pop tune, Suzi. Sometimes they sound alike."

"Then why did Brian get me fired?" Suzi demanded.

"They're two separate issues, Suzi," Marcus said, sighing in frustration.

"It's true I complained to Marcus about some of the dance steps you taught us," Brian said carefully. Then he shrugged. "We thought we'd try out a new choreographer."

"So you *did* have me fired!" Suzi cried.

"Because we wanted a change, not because we wanted to get away with stealing your song," Marcus said, trying to calm her down.

"And I didn't give your tape to anyone either," Brian continued. "Call my housekeeper if you don't believe me. She picks up that stupid cassette and dusts under it every week!"

Suzi narrowed her eyes. "You'd better come clean with me, Brian Beat. Or else!" With that, Suzi skated back up the aisle. The back doors to the theater slammed behind her.

"Whew!" Marcus said. "If that isn't enough excitement for one day. Okay, people. Show's over."

"Think we should follow her?" Joe asked his brother.

Frank shook his head. "We don't have any real evidence against her. Not yet, anyway. Let's wait and see what we can learn from the sound crew."

37

Up on the stage, Marcus ran his hands over his face. He looked frazzled and a bit stunned. "Brian, I really think we need to get a doctor in here to see you."

"I'm fine, really," Brian insisted. "Look, I'll prove it." He spun around and did the double-time step Jason had invented. The crew laughed, and the extras broke into applause.

Suddenly Mindy Beckett appeared from the wing. Her face was ashen and her eyes were wide. The crew took one look at her and stopped laughing. The extras fell silent.

"Brian," she said in a quiet voice, "we just got a phone call from your hometown. It's . . . it's bad news."

Brian stopped dancing and his smile disappeared. "What's wrong?" he asked anxiously.

"There's been an accident," Mindy said, swallowing hard. "Oh, Brian, I'm so sorry."

"Tell me," Brian said, his fists clenched by his side.

"It's your mother," Mindy said. "She's been in a car accident. And she's hurt."

5 Bad News

Joe watched as Brian went pale and almost crumpled at the news. Immediately Jason was at his side, holding his friend up with a supportive arm.

"Look, buddy, it's going to be all right," Jason said. "You've got to be with her, that's all."

Frank spoke up. "Is there any news about her condition?" he asked gently.

Mindy shook her head sadly. "No. Just that she's been taken to Ositos Community Hospital."

"I'm going," Brian said firmly. "I can't take staying here, not knowing how she is." Brian turned to Marcus, who was distracted and obviously upset.

"Marcus, shut the production down," Brian said with conviction. I'm going to Ositos right now."

Marcus opened his mouth, then closed it again. Finally, he let out a weary sigh. "That's it, folks," he told Lenny Wiseman and the crew. "I'll call you when we get back to town."

Lenny just sat there openmouthed. Then he held out his arms and told the crew, "Take a week. Take a month. Take as long as you want, people. We're shutting down."

"What do you mean we?" Brian asked Marcus. "You don't need to come with me."

"Oh, yes I do," Marcus replied. "As soon as this leaks to the public—and believe me, it will—the hospital will be crawling with screaming girls. You'll need me to run interference for you."

"Yeah, I guess you're right," Brian admitted.

"I'm coming, too," Jason said. "If you don't mind, that is. Your mother is like family to me. Anyhow, you're bound to need some moral support."

"Thanks, man," Brian said, squeezing Jason's shoulder. He turned to Marcus. "Call the airport. Find out when the next flight to Palm Springs is."

"I came here in my limo," Marcus answered. "We'll head out to the airport and make our reservations on the car phone."

Brian nodded. "Good idea. Thanks, Marcus. You're always here for me when I need you."

Joe sensed that Marcus was relieved that Brian was so appreciative. "You bet I am."

Then Brian turned to Frank and Joe. "I could use you guys, too, if you don't mind coming along."

"No problem," Joe said eagerly. "You know we want to help. We can help Marcus run interference. Think of us as your professional bodyguards." Joe made a muscle. "At your service, Mr. Beat."

Brian smiled for the first time since Mindy gave him the news about his mother. His green eyes sparkled as he said, "Thanks, guys. I owe you—big time."

While Brian changed his clothes, Joe called his parents and explained what was going on. Being a private investigator himself, Mr. Hardy had no trouble understanding his sons' situation. "Keep us posted on your whereabouts," he said. "And be careful."

"We will, Dad," Joe replied. "Thanks!"

Marcus's white limousine was waiting in the alley behind the theater. Marcus and Jason were already inside, sipping mineral water taken from the built-in bar. Brian, Frank, and Joe piled in, and the driver took off for the airport.

An hour and a half later, Frank, Joe, Brian, Jason, and Marcus were sitting in the first-class section of an airplane flying over the Mojave desert. The five of them had the first-class area to themselves, and since the flight attendants had immediately recognized Brian and Jason, they were getting the royal treatment.

"Can I get you another pillow, Mr. Beat?" an auburn-haired attendant asked.

"No, thanks," Brian replied. "I'm fine."

"How about a drink? Or a snack?" a male attendant asked.

"No, really," Brian answered.

Joe watched Brian blush and pretend to be falling asleep so that the flight attendants would leave him alone. The Hardys were sitting across the aisle from Brian, and Jason and Marcus were in the row behind, taking a nap. After the attendants left, Brian scooted across the aisle to sit with Joe and Frank.

"Must be tough," Joe said, grinning.

Brian frowned. "I still can't get used to being a celebrity. Like that scene with Suzi B. It seems that when you're famous, people think they can accuse you of all sorts of things. I never even had time to listen to her tape!" Brian said in frustration. "So how could she think I stole her song?"

"But you did fire her," Joe put in.

"Marcus and I let her go," Brian said. "It was a joint decision."

Frank was deep in thought as he looked out the plane's window. The California desert appeared far below, surrounded by snowcapped mountains.

"Suzi B. could have a real grudge against you," Frank said.

"Enough to hurt you," Joe added.

Brian sighed. "I just can't believe all this is

happening," he said. "Back in the beginning, the group was such a blast. We used to sing at parties and in talent shows. No money, but we sure had fun."

"How did you get started?" Joe asked, curious.

"It was Jason's idea. We both play guitar, and we used to jam together. One day we were hanging around my house and he said, 'Let's start a band.' So we did." Brian shrugged. "Or I guess I should say he did."

"What do you mean?" Frank asked.

"Once Jason decided to start a band," Brian said, "he got very serious about it. He set up rehearsal times, he picked out songs for us to learn, he auditioned other singers. That's how we found J.T. and Terry."

"And look where you are today," Frank said.

Brian nodded. "Jason used to be the lead singer. But then Marcus came along. He was a deejay at a radio station in Palm Springs, and he managed a few local bands on the side. He told us he could take us all the way to the top of the charts. So we signed a contract." Brian gazed out the window, remembering. "The first thing he did was make me lead singer."

"Wow!" Joe exclaimed. "How did you like that?"

"At first I resisted. I didn't want to hurt Jason. But after a while, I got into it—not the stardom stuff so much, but the music. I even started writing songs and working on my singing."

"And what about Jason?" Frank asked. "How did he feel about the whole thing?"

"Surprised," said a voice. Joe looked up to see Jason standing in the aisle behind Joe. The teen was rubbing the sleep out of his eyes. "But you know what? Marcus was right. Brian has the looks, the voice, the moves. We wouldn't have made it this far without him out front."

"Thanks, man," Brian said self-consciously.

"Besides, what do I have to complain about?" Jason added. "Marcus said he'd make us stars, and he did. Who could ask for more than that?"

"Brian, baby," a smooth, syrupy voice cooed, "how ya doin'?"

They all turned to find Pico Hernandez standing in the aisle with a pen and a pad of paper in his hands. Joe stood up to block Pico's path.

"How'd you get in here?" Frank demanded.

Pico sneered at Frank, ignoring his question. Instead, he elbowed his way past Joe and Jason and planted himself in front of Brian. "Mind if I ask you a few questions?"

"You bet I mind," Brian said. He looked across the aisle at Marcus, who was sleeping soundly.

"I could call a flight attendant and have this weasel thrown out of first class," Joe offered.

"But, Brian," Pico said with a hurt expression, "I'm doing you a favor. If you give me an exclusive interview, I promise I won't alert the media in Palm

44

Springs. But if you don't . . . well, I'm afraid it's going to a real circus."

Joe and Frank were standing by, ready to throw Pico out. But Brian threw up his hands in exasperation and said, "All right, all right. Five minutes, that's it. Then buzz off."

Frank and Joe sat back down in their seats while Brian and Jason sat across the aisle and gave Pico his interview.

"What a pushy guy," Frank remarked quietly, his eyes on Pico.

"Sneaky, too," Joe said. "I get the feeling he'd do pretty much anything to uncover a juicy bit of celebrity gossip."

"Or maybe even make something juicy happen just so he'd have a story," Frank said.

"What do you mean?" Joe asked.

Frank reminded Joe that Pico had been backstage at the Rialto. "You don't think he caused that accident," Joe said, "just so he'd be the first one with the story?"

"Pico already started that rumor about Brian not signing with Marcus," Frank pointed out.

"But that's gossip," Joe said. "What you're talking about goes a lot further."

"You're right," Frank acknowledged. "But I say we keep an eye on the guy, and see if he's around if another so-called accident occurs."

Brian and Jason finished giving their interview.

Marcus woke up just as Pico was reluctantly returning to his seat in coach. The manager gave Pico a look, and Brian quickly explained why he and Jason bothered to speak to the reporter.

"Let's hope he doesn't notify the press that you'll be at the hospital," Marcus said. "Or else we could have another mob scene on our hands."

Minutes later the plane touched down and taxied to the terminal. Thanks to Marcus, a limo was waiting to take them all to the hospital.

The drive to Ositos took them out of Palm Springs and across the Mojave. Frank and Joe gazed with awe at the miles and miles of dry land, covered only with cactus, scrub brush, and rocks. After about thirty miles, the flatness changed to grassy hills. Beyond the hills were pine-covered mountains. Throughout the drive, Brian said nothing. From the worried look on his face, it was obvious he was thinking about his mother.

"Amazing scenery," Joe said, trying to distract Brian.

"Those are the San Bernardino Mountains," Brian replied, suddenly coming to life. "Ositos is in the foothills. It's a beautiful place."

"Beautiful, but boring," Jason said. "Believe me, when I left for L.A. I never looked back."

The limo turned off the highway and drove down a succession of back roads. Eventually, the driver pulled up in front of the hospital.

"Oh no," Brian said, his head in his hands.

"What's wrong?" Joe asked.

"Look," Brian said, grimly pointing out the limo window.

The front steps of the hospital were crawling with excited teenagers. Standing among them was Pico Hernandez, grinning from ear to ear.

"So much for Pico's word," Marcus said with contempt.

"What I want to know is how Pico Hernandez got here so fast," Joe muttered.

"He's a vulture," Jason quipped. "He probably flew."

"I'll give him a few quotes and keep him off your back," Marcus said. "Frank, Joe, make a path for Brian. Get him inside the hospital however you can."

"We'll do our best," Frank said.

Marcus threw open the limousine door. Immediately the crowd surged forward. Frank and Joe leaped out and used their bodies to open a pathway through the shrieking mob for Brian and Jason. Marcus intercepted Pico and led him away from the stairs.

The screaming fans followed Brian, Joe, Frank, and Jason right up to the hospital doors. There, a security guard helped them inside and closed the doors on the mob.

"You must be some star," the guard said, wiping his brow. "I've never seen a crowd like that."

"Thanks for your help," Joe told the man.

Inside the hospital, Brian found out his mother's room number, and soon the four teens were standing outside a room on the second floor. Brian knocked softly on the door, and a dark-haired woman in a blue dress and white coat emerged.

Brian introduced himself and the woman said, "I'm Dr. Fisher. I'm happy to say we have good news. Your mother only sustained minor cuts and bruises and a mild concussion. She's awake now, and you can visit with her for a few minutes."

Joe saw Brian let out a relieved sigh. The teen's body visibly relaxed. "Thanks, Doc," Brian said with a smile. "Lead the way."

While Brian went inside with the doctor, Joe and Frank remained in the hall. Jason paced the floor nervously, then paused and said, "If there's one thing I can't stand, it's waiting. I'm going to find a cup of coffee. See you in a minute."

Joe noticed the label on the door read Bettencourt. He pointed it out to Frank. "That must be Brian's real last name."

"You mean it's not Beat?" Frank joked.

A few minutes later, the door opened and Brian appeared. "Hey, guys," he began.

Just then a hospital orderly in green scrubs and a mask came running around the corner at top speed, pushing a cart full of bottles and cups in front of him. Suddenly he veered right. His cart swerved toward Frank, Joe, and Brian.

48

"Hey!" Joe cried out. "Watch what you're doing."

But the orderly didn't hear, or at least he didn't care. He kept on coming, right at them. With a gasp of surprise, Frank and Joe jumped out of the way. Brian was left alone at the open door. Quickly, the orderly reached down to his cart, picked up a vial of liquid, and tossed it—right at Brian's face!

Brian let out a scream of pain, put his hands to his face, and stumbled backward through the open door.

6 Disorderly Conduct

Frank reached out to grab Brian, to prevent his fall through the doorway, but Brian went sprawling anyway.

"Brian!" his mother cried, sitting up in her bed.

Joe saw the orderly taking off down the hall. "We can't let him get away!" he shouted.

"I'll take care of Brian," Frank said. "You go after the orderly."

Joe nodded and ran down the hall. Frank knelt beside Brian and pulled his hands away from his face. There were two ugly red splotches on his neck and another one on his cheek. Luckily the assailant missed Brian's eyes.

Thinking fast, Frank grabbed Brian under his

arms and lifted him to his feet. "We have to rinse this stuff off your face," Frank said urgently.

As his hands touched Brian's sweatshirt, Frank felt something cold. He looked down and realized that whatever the orderly had tossed on Brian's face also landed on his sweatshirt. And it had frozen there!

Quickly Frank led Brian to the lavatory inside Mrs. Bettencourt's room.

"What is it?" Brian asked, gingerly touching his face and wincing. "What happened?"

"My guess is someone threw liquid nitrogen on your face," Frank said. He pointed to Brian's sweatshirt. "It's the only thing that freezes up like this when it solidifies. We've got to rinse it off your face before it does serious damage. Put your face under the faucet."

Brian did as he was told, and Frank turned on the water. A moment later, Dr. Fisher ran into the lavatory, followed by Marcus.

"What happened?" the doctor asked.

Frank filled her in on the details as she bent over the shaken teen. Marcus got a shocked and worried look on his face, and he also leaned over to make sure Brian was okay.

"Did I do the right thing?" Frank asked.

"Absolutely," Dr. Fisher said. "You're right about this being liquid nitrogen," she added, examining Brian's face gingerly. "It's used to remove warts and other skin lesions. It freezes the skin, which is what it did to Brian's shirt and face. Any orderly would be able to find it and know what it was."

"Is he going to be all right?" Marcus asked, obviously concerned. "Any permanent scarring?"

"It's unlikely," Dr. Fisher said. "The warm air in the room halted the freezing process, and the water will wash away any liquid nitrogen residue." She leaned down to Brian, who still had his face under running water. "Stay there another couple of minutes," she said. "Then we'll put a topical cream on the injured areas to help the healing process."

"Brian, are you okay?" Brian's mother called. Frank looked up. Mrs. Bettencourt had gotten out of bed and was walking toward the lavatory.

Frank hurried toward her and introduced himself. Then he helped Brian's mother back into bed and explained what had happened. She looked frightened and confused, and Frank knew the double shock of the car accident and Brian's injury was taking its toll on her.

"Lie down," Frank told her gently. "He's going to be all right."

A few minutes later, Joe returned to Mrs. Bettencourt's room to discover a nurse applying cream to Brian's wounds. Marcus was pacing the room, and Jason was sitting in a chair by the window.

"You're lucky," Dr. Fisher was saying. "Most of the liquid nitrogen landed on your shirt."

"Can he work?" Marcus asked. "We're right in the middle of filming a video."

"Certainly," she replied. "Just give his face a day or two to heal."

Frank joined Joe in the doorway. "No luck?"

Joe shook his head. "The guy just took off. But we should notify hospital security and see if they can find any clues."

"Dr. Fisher's already phoned security," Frank told him. "Every hospital worker is being asked to account for his or her whereabouts in the past hour."

"That's great, but what if it's not someone who works here?" Joe suggested. At Frank's surprised look, Joe pulled him farther away from the room. "What if it's Marcus? Or even Pico?" he asked quietly.

Frank thought for a moment. "Could be. But we can't just ask them outright, can we?"

"Not exactly," Joe agreed. "When Marcus showed up, was he out of breath or anything?"

"Nope," said Frank.

"What about Jason?" Joe asked.

Frank shook his head no.

Both Hardys looked over to Marcus and Jason. Brian was trying to give them and his mother a reassuring smile, but the pain in his face was evident.

"This is a serious stunt," Joe said. "If Pico's behind it, we're sure to see him turn up soon."

"Brian," Dr. Fisher said softly, "your mother has been through a lot today. I think it would be best if you left now. I'll give her a sedative so she can sleep."

"Can I come back tomorrow?" Brian asked.

"No way," Marcus broke in. "There's a lunatic in this hospital, and I'm not giving him a second chance to get near you. I want to report this to the police and then head back to L.A."

"But what about my mom?" Brian insisted.

"She's going to be fine," Dr. Fisher said. "Barring any changes in her condition, she'll be going home tomorrow."

"All right," Brian said reluctantly. "If you think it's best."

Jason and Marcus waited in the hall while Brian said goodbye to his mother. Frank and Joe took Dr. Fisher aside and discussed the situation with her. She assured them that the hospital would pursue a full investigation.

"Let us know if anything turns up," Joe said firmly. He explained quietly how this wasn't the first of Brian's accidents.

The doctor's face showed concern. "Take care of him," she said. "I can see he's in safe hands with you two."

Frank thanked her. Brian came out of his mother's room then, looking pale and worried. Marcus led everyone outside and through the mob of waiting fans. A horde of reporters and TV cameramen had joined them. Joe noticed right away that Pico had a front and center spot.

"Brian!" he cried out. "Brian Beat! What happened to your face?"

Pico snapped a photo of Brian holding up his hands to protect his face.

"Buzz off, Pico," Joe said, pushing the reporter away. "Leave the kid alone!"

Joe and Frank hurried Brian inside the limo, followed by the others, and the car sped off down the desert road.

The next morning, Frank and Joe were on their way to Magic World, along with their parents, Mr. Manstroni and his two children, and their Aunt Gertrude. The night before, Frank and Joe told their father they'd be staying on in California as long as Brian's attacker was still on the loose.

Brian had invited them all to spend the day with him at the area's largest amusement park, Magic World. As the Hardys and their friends drove into the parking lot, Brian was waiting for them at the front gate, wearing a big pair of sunglasses and a fake mustache.

"I hope your disguise works better this time than that day we met you at the video arcade," Joe joked.

Brian laughed and his mustache wiggled. "I hope so, too. Or else you guys will have another chance at being professional bodyguards."

Joe introduced Brian to his parents and his Aunt Gertrude and then to Harold Manstroni and his awestruck children.

"Pleased to meet you all," Brian said politely. Then his eyes sparkled and he said, "I don't know about you, but I'm psyched! Magic World has got to be one of the greatest places on earth. Let's do it."

Almost at a run, Brian led the way to the main entrance. Soon they were all strolling through Magic World. The park, which was set among the rolling hills east of Los Angeles, was packed with families. There were long lines for every ride, but from the delirious looks of the people getting off the rides, the wait was worth it.

"This is incredible!" Joe exclaimed. "I can't decide which ride to take first."

"Hey," Brian cried suddenly, "there's Raging Tunnel! I love that ride!"

Joe knew that Raging Tunnel was Magic World's most famous ride. It was a roller coaster enclosed in a dark tunnel illuminated only with colorful neon lights.

"Well, let's do it," Frank said.

"Oh, dear, do you think you should?" Aunt Gertrude said anxiously. "It could be pretty dangerous."

"Gertrude, you worry too much," Laura Hardy

said, smiling gently. "These rides are all perfectly safe. Why else would they let people on them?"

"Exactly," Fenton agreed. "Let's all do it!"

The Manstroni kids yelped with glee, and the whole group lined up to take the ride. It was a long wait, but finally Frank, Joe, and Brian were at the head of the line.

A young woman checked their tickets, and then let them in. Then she cut off the rest of the group, saying, "That's all for this ride. There are only two cars left. The rest of you will have to wait for the next set of cars."

The Hardys and the Manstronis looked disappointed, but Mr. Hardy urged the three boys to go ahead.

"We'll meet you at the exit," he said.

Brian climbed in on car, with Frank and Joe in the car behind him. The attendant came over to buckle their seat belts. "Keep your hands in the cars," he said. "And have fun, guys."

With a churning of gears, the cars began to move forward on the narrow track. Suddenly, they gained speed and plunged into the black tunnel. Frank, Joe, and Brian let out whoops as their cars flew down hills and around curves. Wild neon lights blurred past them, creating a kaleidoscope of colors.

Suddenly Joe heard a loud grinding of gears, followed by a sharp crack. Frank and Joe stared into the darkness, trying to figure out what was going on.

"What's wrong?" Frank said to Joe.

In front of them, Brian's car wobbled sideways. Brian turned around and gave Frank and Joe a horrified look.

"Help!" he cried. "Something's wrong with the ride!"

The next moment, Joe watched, helpless, as Brian's car wobbled so much, it careened off the rails.

"Do something!" While Brian cried out, the car he was riding in skittered toward the wall at breakneck speed. And Frank and Joe were about to go next!

7 Way Off Track

Frank heard Brian scream as his car hit the wall, tipped over, and stopped. Frank and Joe's car came next. It hit the back wheel of Brian's car, which was sticking out onto the tracks, derailed, and tipped over. Immediately, the neon lights went off, an emergency spotlight came on, and a siren began to wail.

Lying in his overturned car, Frank moved his arms, legs, and head, checking for injuries. As far as he could tell, he was unharmed, so he unbuckled his seat belt and climbed out. Joe was doing the same.

Frank figured that since the cars ran individually along the rails, the rest of the group that had gone into the tunnel ahead of them were probably okay.

"You okay?" Joe yelled over the squeal of the siren and the voices of the riders ahead.

"I think so," Frank shouted back. "The seat belts saved us from flying out of the cars."

Together they climbed over to Brian. He was lying in his car, unmoving. "Brian, can you hear me?" Joe shouted.

There was a moment's pause, then Brian stirred. "I'm okay, I think," he said in a trembling voice. "Just a little shaken up."

Frank unbuckled Brian's safety belt and helped him out of the car. Brian was wearing shorts, and Frank saw an ugly gash across the singer's knee. The teen limped as he got out of the car.

"Are you okay?" Frank asked him.

Wincing, Brian nodded his head. "Fine. I think. It hurts a little, but I think I can walk."

The tunnel was so small that none of them could stand up straight. Up ahead, Frank could barely make out the other people who had gone on the ride with them. Several figures were slowly emerging from their cars and making their way toward the end of the ride.

"Someone turn on the lights," a young woman cried in the dark. "Please!"

Frank led the way toward the exit. Within twenty feet he encountered the first stranded car. A mother and her two young children sat there, obviously scared half to death.

"What's happening?" the little girl asked. "Did somebody break the ride?"

"We're not sure," Frank said. "But stay right here, and we'll get someone to fix it."

The three boys continued in the direction of the exit. Halfway there, they were met by two members of the Magic World security team. "Are you all right?" one of them called.

"We're fine," Frank shouted. "But you've got to get these people out of here. They're all pretty scared." One of the security men nodded and continued into the tunnel. The other one insisted on escorting the trio the rest of the way.

Mr. and Mrs. Hardy, Aunt Gertrude, and Mr. Manstroni were waiting, concerned expressions on their faces. "I knew it," Aunt Gertrude said. "I knew that thing was dangerous!"

There were several other security men standing at the ride's exit. A control booth stood nearby, and Frank could see a mechanic inside, obviously trying to figure out what went wrong.

One of the security men, a middle-aged man with a mustache, asked, "What happened?"

"We don't know," Joe said. "We were going along just fine, and suddenly the cars derailed."

"I want to check out that control booth," Frank said.

Inside the booth, a man dressed in blue coveralls sat sprawled in a chair. A mechanic stood at a

61

display terminal, punching in commands at the keyboard.

"What happened?" Frank asked.

"I . . . I don't know," the man in the coveralls answered, looking around him uncertainly. "I was monitoring the ride the way I always do. Then something hit me on the back of the head and everything went blank."

"The system has been tampered with," the mechanic said at last. "Look at this."

The man, whose name tag read Rich, pointed to the screen. "System Terminated," Frank read aloud. "How?" he wanted to know.

Rich scanned the display. "Whoever knocked out Roger here just happened to know what switch to throw to shut off the program that runs this ride. If you guess the right switch, bingo! The ride's over."

"But if you throw the switch while someone's still in the tunnel, their car could derail?" Joe asked.

"You bet," Roger said wearily. "But in ten years working here, this has never happened to me."

"Brian Beat has never been on your ride," Frank said under his breath. "Did you see your attacker?"

Roger shook his head and rubbed the back of his neck. "I sure wish I did, but unfortunately no. I was standing at the board, watching the display. Then, pow! I was out like a light."

"We'll have to question the attendants," Joe put in. "Find out if they saw anyone suspicious hanging out around the control booth."

"Good idea," Frank agreed.

"I can't believe this is happening," Brian said. "Why me?"

"I don't know," Frank said. "But we're going to find out. And that's a promise."

The group spent the rest of the morning at Magic World, answering questions for the security staff. Brian had his knee bandaged by a nurse after the management also insisted that Frank, Joe, and Brian be checked out by Magic World's first aid staff. Finally, the president of Magic World insisted on buying them lunch. Before they left, he assured Frank and Joe that he'd do a full investigation of the incident. Then he told them they were all welcome back at the park anytime, free of charge.

Frank and Joe spent the rest of the day with their parents, taking in a few last sights before the Hardys and Aunt Gertrude had to return to Bayport. Brian went along, since Frank and Joe didn't want him out of their sight.

Fortunately, there were no more incidents, and the next morning Frank and Joe saw their family off at the airport. Then the boys drove their rental car to the Santa Monica beach pier, where the Funky Four were shooting a Jet Ski scene for the "Can't Catch Me" video.

"This rental car is so boring," Joe complained as Frank parked the silver four-door sedan their parents had rented. "I wish we had a Porsche like Brian drives."

"Dream on, little brother," Frank laughed. "Just be glad we've got wheels, period."

They got out of the car and looked around. The entire area—the pier, the beach around it, and the grassy park above the beach—had been taken over by the video crew. The parking lot was roped off from the rest of the shoot, and private security guards stood behind orange barriers to keep fans and passersby out of the area. There were also several Los Angeles police officers keeping an eye on things. Down on the beach, Lenny Wiseman and the crew were setting up cameras, reflectors, and speakers. Five red and black Jet Skis were parked along the edge of the water.

Frank and Joe got past security by showing them the passes Brian had given them the day before. They strolled past the film crew and recognized some of the extras from the shoot at the Rialto. They were trying to find Brian's name on one of the many trailers set up in the park when a door to one of them popped open and Brian himself appeared.

"Hi, guys," he said. Frank noticed that the red splotches on his face were almost completely healed. "Did you see all the police?" Brian asked. "Marcus called them and reported everything that's been going on. They must have asked me a million questions."

Frank saw this was a perfect opportunity for them to ask Brian some of their own. "Can we come inside?" he asked.

"Sure," Brian said. "What's up?"

"After that accident at the park yesterday," Frank said, sitting down on one of the bench seats inside the trailer, "we need to evaluate who our suspects are, and why."

"First," Joe said, "there's Suzi B."

"I don't think she's mad enough to want to kill me," Brian remarked. "Besides, I doubt Suzi B. is capable of rewiring a microphone. She's a great dancer, but she's not exactly mechanically inclined."

"Then she probably didn't knock out the operator at Raging Tunnel and mess with the controls," Frank pointed out.

Brian knocked his palm to the side of his head. "I can't believe I forgot to tell you."

"What?" Joe asked.

"Remember that cassette tape Suzi B. gave me?" Brian asked. When Frank nodded, he went on. "I looked for it when I came back from Ositos. It's gone. My housekeeper says she hasn't seen it for at least a month."

"And you're sure you didn't move it?" Joe asked.

"I looked everywhere. Besides, I've hardly been home lately. And till just recently we've been on tour."

"Is there anyone else who's had access to the cassette?" Frank asked.

"Just my housekeeper," Brian answered. "And

Jason, J.T., and Terry. They're the only ones who have been to my house in the last few weeks."

Just then, there was a knock on the door. Brian went to answer it, and Marcus appeared, looking stern. "Brian, I'd like a word with you. In my trailer, please. I want you boys to come, too," he told Frank and Joe.

The three boys followed Marcus across the park to his trailer. Brian limped the whole way, and Frank realized that his knee was probably still bothering him. They stepped inside and Marcus shut the door.

"Brian," the manager began in a strangely quiet voice, "you lied to me. You told me you were planning to sign a new contract with me next month."

"But I am," Brian said simply.

"Then why did you arrange a meeting with Harold Manstroni yesterday? He's trying to sign you, isn't he?" Marcus grabbed a copy of *Dance Party Scene* from his desk and shoved it at Brian.

On the front cover of the magazine was a photograph, taken from a distance and out of focus. But in it, Frank clearly recognized Brian, the Hardys, and Harold Manstroni.

"That must have been taken yesterday, at Magic World!" Joe cried out, looking over Frank's shoulder. "But how . . . ?"

"Pico Rodriguez," Frank said. "That toad must follow us everywhere."

Brian saw the picture and laughed. "Marcus, we weren't having a meeting. We were spending the morning at Magic World. Besides, I had no idea Harold Manstroni was going to be there. He's a friend of Frank and Joe's family, that's all."

Marcus grabbed the magazine out of Frank's hand. "Harold Manstroni is one of the most powerful personal managers in the music business."

"We know," Frank said. "But he really is our parents' friend. My father met him years ago in college."

"I don't believe it," Marcus snapped. "And I don't believe Brian just happened to meet you two in a video arcade, either." He scowled. "Who are you guys? Harold Manstroni's assistants?"

Brian burst out laughing. "Get real, Marcus. Frank and Joe are my friends. They don't work for anybody."

Marcus looked uncomfortable for a moment. Frank saw he must have realized how foolish he seemed, accusing him and Joe of being Manstroni's assistants.

The manager swallowed, then smiled awkwardly. "Listen," he said. "I'm sorry. I guess I'm under a lot of pressure here. I just need to know that you trust me, that you believe in me. I'm looking out for you, Brian, and I always have. You know that, right?"

"Right," Brian agreed.

While Marcus and Brian settled their differences,

Frank looked around the trailer. His eyes lit on a cassette lying on Marcus's desk. The label stuck to the tape read SONGS BY JASON. Intrigued, Frank stepped closer to the table. While Marcus was showing Brian the newest press packet he'd prepared, Frank pocketed the tape.

There was a knock on the door, and a crew member's voice called out, "Ten minutes. Everyone on the set in ten minutes."

"Gotta run," Brian said. "Come on, guys."

Together, the three friends walked back to Brian's trailer. "I need to finish changing into my costume," he said.

Brian opened the door of the trailer and stepped inside. Suddenly he stopped dead and let out a gasp.

"What's wrong?" Frank asked, hurrying up behind him.

"Look," he said, pointing at his dressing table mirror.

Frank and Joe looked. The mirror was plastered with newspaper and magazine clippings, all of Brian. BRIAN BEAT'S EGO OUT OF CONTROL read one of them. DANCE MUSIC STAR GETS SWELLED HEAD read another.

But the biggest picture of all was one of Brian's face, which had been ripped out of a magazine and stuck to the wall. Over it, someone had drawn a bull's-eye. Under it were the words "Can't Catch Me!"

8 Wipe Out!

Brian's face turned bright red, and he snatched the picture off the wall. He crumpled it into a ball and threw it against the mirror.

"Take it easy," Joe said. "Try not to let it get to you."

Brian made his hand into a fist and was about to punch out the wall.

"Chill out," Frank urged. "We'll find out who did this."

Joe took a look around the trailer. The whole place was trashed. The bench seats had been pulled out. The contents of Brian's duffel bag were scattered on the ground. There were papers and magazines all over the floor, and all his CDs and cassettes were thrown out of their cases.

69

"I think someone was looking for something here," Joe remarked.

"Suzi B.?" Frank guessed.

Brian's eyes flashed. "You think she did this?" he asked, surprised.

"Why not?" Joe said. "What if she broke in here, looking for her tape, and decided to leave the threatening note, too?"

"It's a possibility," Frank said. He went over to the mirror to read the magazine articles. "On the other hand, every one of these stories comes from *Dance Party Scene.*"

"So you think it could have been Pico?" Joe said.

"It wouldn't surprise me," Brian said with a grimace. "This kind of garbage sells magazines. And Pico is a worm—he loves dirt." Brian ripped another article off the mirror and crumpled it in his fist.

Frank gazed thoughtfully at the mirror. "Either way, if it's Pico or Suzi B., it doesn't seem as if Brian's mysterious enemy is out to kill him. He just wants to harass him."

"What do you mean?" Brian asked.

"If someone was really trying to kill you, I think he would have succeeded by now," Frank said. "But after all the accidents, you've come through with nothing more than a few cuts and bruises."

Joe nodded. "It's more like your enemy is trying to pay you back for something you did to him—or her."

70

"If that's true, the evidence sure does point to Suzi B.," Frank said.

Joe thought for a moment. "Who else would want revenge against Brian?" Then it came to him. "Marcus!" he said in excitement.

"Marcus?" Frank said, surprised.

Brian shook his head and blinked his eyes. "Now that's coming out of left field," he said. "Maybe you should just stick to being my bodyguard!"

Joe laughed, and then said, "No, really. Think about it. If Marcus is worried that you're planning to sign with another manager, he might be mad enough to want revenge. Or else he could be trying to scare you into sticking with him. See how reassuring Marcus has been all this time?"

"I think I see where you're headed," Frank said. "Marcus could be hoping that Brian will get upset about these accidents. So upset that he thinks Marcus is the only one he can trust."

"But I *am* going to sign with Marcus," Brian said in frustration.

"Marcus obviously isn't convinced," Joe said.

Brian ran his hands over his face. "I don't know what to think anymore," he said wearily.

Just then, there was a knock on the door. "Brian, they need you on the beach," Mindy Beckett called. "Lenny wants to shoot some close-ups of the Funky Four on the Jet Skis."

Brian quickly changed into a sleek purple and black wet suit and headed down to the beach. Joe

71

and Frank followed, discussing their next move in the investigation.

"Keep your eyes out for Pico," Frank urged. "And Suzi B. If either of them sneaked into Brian's trailer, they might still be hanging around."

Joe nodded.

Jason, J.T., and Terry were already on the set, dressed in solid purple wet suits. While Lenny Wiseman filmed close-ups of the Funky Four hopping on the Jet Skis and riding across the water, Frank and Joe took a quick tour of the set, looking for a sign of Suzi B. or Pico.

"Everything seems cool," Joe said as they covered the last corner. "Let's head back to where Brian is and watch the filming."

"Okay, that's it for the close-ups," Lenny was announcing as the Hardys approached. "Now it's time for the action shots. In this scene, Brian will be heading for the pier with the villain and her three henchman on his tail. At the last second, Brian releases the Jet Ski handlebars, lowering them, and rides under the pier to escape the bad guys."

"Does that mean you don't need us for a while?" Jason asked, sounding a little disappointed.

"Right," Lenny replied. "You, J.T., and Terry are free until this afternoon."

"Cool," Terry said. "Let's head into Santa Monica to grab a bite."

"Sounds good to me," Jason said reluctantly.

"Catch you guys later." With that, Jason, J.T., and Terry walked up the beach.

Brian—who was still favoring his injured leg—jumped onto a waiting Jet Ski. "Let's do it," he said eagerly.

"Not so fast, hotshot," Marcus said, heading over to him. "That knee of yours is still bothering you, I can tell. Besides, after everything that's happened lately, I'd be crazy to let you near that pier. We're going to use a stunt double to play you."

"Aw, come on," Brian pleaded. "I want to have some fun. My knee's fine."

"You're sitting this scene out," Marcus said, his hands on his hips. "And that's final."

Joe walked over and put his hand on Brian's shoulder. "I know it's a drag," he said. "But Marcus is right this time. Don't push your luck."

"Oh, all right," Brian said irritably, getting off the ski.

"Joe," Mindy Beckett said, "you're about the same size as Brian, and your hair is almost the same color. Think you can drive a Jet Ski under the pier?"

"You bet!" Joe exclaimed.

"And Frank, how would you like to play one of the henchmen?"

"One bad guy at your service," he replied.

Mindy gave them their costumes, and they quickly dashed off to a trailer to change. Joe wore a

73

purple and black wet suit to match Brian, while Frank had on a solid black one. They returned to the beach, and Joe hopped on the Jet Ski Brian had planned to ride. It had a distinctive blue and purple marking to stand out in the video. All the villains' skis were painted solid black.

"You better check out that thing before you ride it," Frank advised. "Be sure no one's tampered with it."

Joe nodded and ran a quick check of the Jet Ski. He did a test run out in the waves and zoomed back into shore.

"Seems okay to me," he said, coming to a stop in a wave of spray. "Let's do it!"

Frank was standing by with the actors who were playing the villains. A young girl with long red hair named Marcella was dressed in a black wet suit. So were the three burly stuntmen who were playing her henchmen. Three camera operators were going to film the action—one from the pier, one from the beach, and one from a small motorboat out in the water.

Lenny gathered the actors together and explained what was going to happen. "Joe will drive parallel to the beach in the direction of the pier. We'll take wide shots of Joe, and later we can intercut them with close-ups of Brian on the Jet Ski.

"The henchmen will follow Joe about fifty yards back," Lenny continued. "Marcella will be in the lead with the three henchmen riding behind in a

74

V-shape formation. About halfway across the bay, I want the bad guys to begin gaining on Joe. By the time he reaches the pier, they should be no more than fifty feet back. Then Joe goes under the pier right below where the camera operator is standing. Marcella and her men veer off to the right and miss the pier completely. Got it?" He let it all sink in. "Okay, let's try it."

They all started their Jet Skis. Lenny picked up his walkie-talkie, which he used to communicate with the camera crew.

"Action!" he shouted, first into a walkie-talkie, then at the actors.

Joe took off across the water. The wind blew against his face, and spray flew up from the Jet Ski. Joe's heart was racing. He couldn't believe he was filming a video! He remembered he should act, so he turned around to see the bad guys following. The henchmen got closer. Then Joe saw himself getting closer to the pier. It was supported by a series of heavy wooden pilings with two crossed steel rods bolted between them.

Joe saw the camera operator standing on the pier between the second and third pilings from the end. As Joe drove toward the pilings, he released the handlebars, ducked his head, and maneuvered the Jet Ski under the steel rods and between the pilings. It was a tough move, since there wasn't a lot of room to steer the Jet Ski, and the handlebars were down around his stomach. But in a few swift moves, Joe had steered between the pilings and come out on the other side of the pier.

"All right!" he shouted.

The camerawoman waved at him from the pier and cried, "Looks great!"

Thrilled, Joe circled around and headed back to shore. Marcella and her henchmen were already on their way back.

As they reached the shore, Brian, Marcus, and the crew burst into applause. "Fabulous!" Lenny bubbled. "Perfect! Why rehearse anymore? Let's just do it. Places, everyone," Lenny said. "This is a take." He flipped on his walkie-talkie. "And . . . action!"

Once again, Joe shot across the water with the bad guys on his tail. It felt great to be roaring across the bay. He glanced behind him. Marcella, with her windswept red hair and heavy makeup, looked extremely nasty, and her henchmen in black— Frank included—looked big and dangerous.

Soon the pier loomed before him. Joe tightened his grip on the handlebars and pressed the release button. To his surprise, the handlebars didn't move. He pressed harder. Nothing. The handlebars were locked in an upright position!

With his heart pounding, Joe glanced up at the pier. In a few seconds, he would reach the pilings. If he couldn't lower the handlebars, they would slam into the steel rods and he would crash.

Joe's first instinct was to slow down. He tried to

cut back on the accelerator, but instead of slowing down, the Jet Ski went faster. Joe stared down at the accelerator in horror. It was moving by itself!

Joe looked behind him. Frank and Marcella and her henchmen must have figured out what was wrong. They were veering off to either side of the pier. But Joe didn't have any choice. There was no way he could steer clear at this point. He was too close.

When Joe turned to look forward, what he saw made him gasp. The Jet Ski was plowing across the water at maximum speed—and the pier was only ten feet away!

9 Can't Catch Him

Joe's brain went into overdrive. He knew if he continued on course, he'd smash into the steel crossroads. If he turned left or right, he'd collide with the pilings.

There was only one choice. With a kamikaze scream, he leapt off the back of the Jet Ski. He hit the water with a smack, only five feet away from the third piling. As he came up for air, he saw the Jet Ski plow into the steel crossbars and flip up into the air.

Quickly, he dove underwater and swam down as far as he could go. He covered his head with his hands and hoped the Jet Ski wouldn't land on him. A moment later, he heard the dull sound of the

78

engine running underwater, but the noise was off to his right. Relieved, Joe swam to the surface and took a deep gulp of air.

The Jet Ski was floating on its side a few yards away. Joe treaded water and glanced around. He saw Frank barreling across the bay toward him. Behind him, the other actors had turned around and were heading back to shore. On the beach, Lenny Wiseman was rushing around in an obvious state of panic.

"Are you all right?" Frank called. He cut the engine and cruised up beside Joe.

"A little waterlogged, but otherwise okay," Joe replied, swimming over to Frank's Jet Ski.

"That was some heavy action," Frank said, a worried expression on his face. "What happened?"

"The handlebars locked," Joe said, panting. "I couldn't get the release button to work. Then the accelerator jammed."

"Looks like our saboteur struck again," Frank said with a frown. He steered his Jet Ski closer to Joe, who hopped aboard behind Frank. Then Frank cruised over to where Joe's Jet Ski lay, still running, on its side. "Let's haul your Jet Ski in with us and take a look at it."

As Frank got nearer to the floating Jet Ski, Joe saw something move under the pier. "Hold on," he said, pointing. "What's that?"

Frank glided to a stop and looked. He saw a

half-submerged figure in a black hooded wet suit, clinging to one of the pilings. The person was holding something in his hand.

"Hey!" Joe cried out. "Let's get him," Joe urged his brother.

As soon as Joe called out to him, the stranger in the black wet suit let go of the piling and scrambled onto a blue Jet Ski that was tied up next to him. He started the engine and disappeared out the other side of the pier.

"Hang on, Joe," Frank warned, opening the throttle. Joe wrapped his arms around his brother's waist as Frank steered the Jet Ski under the pier and blasted out the other side.

"There he goes!" Joe cried, pointing toward the stranger, who was roaring away from the pier at top speed.

Frank pushed the Jet Ski as hard as it would go, but the stranger had a healthy one-hundred-yard lead.

When the driver stole a glance over his shoulder, Joe tried to get a look at him, but his brimmed wet suit hood came down over his forehead, casting a shadow across his face.

The stranger faced front again, but as he did, he hit some choppy water and lost his balance. The Jet Ski tipped over, and the rider was flung into the water.

"Let's get him!" Joe shouted over the buzz of the engine. Frank steered across the chop while the stranger swam to his Jet Ski and struggled to climb back on.

"Hurry, Frank!" Joe urged, but he knew they were too late. Their suspect had righted his Jet Ski and was roaring off toward the open ocean.

Frank and Joe followed, flying into the air as they cut across the chop. Suddenly, the stranger veered right and headed toward a gathering of five small sailboats that were gliding peacefully through the water. Frank followed, now only fifty yards behind.

Joe squinted through the spraying water, expecting to see the stranger circle around the sailboats. Instead, he roared between them, sending up a wake that toppled two of the boats and sent the sailors diving into the water.

For his part, Frank swerved around the sailboats, but it was a move he knew would cost him valuable time. As he watched, the hooded stranger shot across the open water to a small speedboat that was anchored beside a floating buoy. The man hopped in, ditching the blue Jet Ski, and roared off.

"That's it," Frank said unhappily. "We can't catch him now."

Joe heaved a disappointed sigh as the speedboat disappeared over the horizon. "But we can ride that Jet Ski back and see if it gives us any clues about who that guy was."

After they checked to make sure the sailors were all right, Joe got on the blue Jet Ski and rode it back to the beach, Frank right behind him. Brian, Marcus, and the crew were waiting for them, along with three Los Angeles policemen.

"What happened?" Marcus cried as they hopped off their Jet Skis. "Are you boys okay?"

"My ski was sabotaged," Joe said. "Whoever did it obviously thought Brian would be riding it."

As Frank continued the story, Joe noticed that the Jet Ski he had been riding for the shoot had been towed in by the crew and was now lying on its side in the sand.

Joe asked a nearby cameraman if he could borrow a screwdriver. The crew member gave him one, and Joe went over to the Jet Ski and opened the engine panel. Everything looked normal until Joe saw a bolt attached under the throttle pin.

"Check this out," Joe called out.

Frank came over and saw what Joe had found. "Someone attached a bolt under the throttle pin and another one inside the handlebar mechanism," Joe explained. "And look here. There's wiring rigged up to the whole thing."

"Phew," Frank said, his eyes wide. "Someone sure went to a lot of trouble this time."

"Someone who knew what he—or she—was doing," Joe confirmed. "The guy under the pier must have used a hand-held remote control device that triggered the bolts to slip into place, jamming the throttle and the handlebars."

Brian was standing next to them now, along with Marcus. The teen star let out a shaky sigh. "Look, guys, I can't take any more of this right now. I'm too stressed out," he said. "I think I'll head over to the gym and work out awhile."

"Wrong," Marcus broke in. "Taping is finished for today, but you're not going anywhere. Nobody is—not until the police ask a few questions."

After answering a uniformed detective's questions about the accident, Frank and Joe went to talk to the head of the prop department, a bearded, balding man named Moe. The Jet Skis had come from a store in Malibu, Moe explained, and had been stored overnight in the prop trailer. Practically everyone in the cast and crew had access to them. As for the Jet Ski that the mysterious figure had abandoned, Joe checked it out but couldn't find any kind of important clue on it. Apparently it had come along with the other skis.

The Hardys were standing in the parking lot waiting for Brian to join them, and all three friends were planning to head over to the gym together.

"Hey, guys!" Brian called. Jason was with him and the two rockers jogged over to join Frank and Joe. "Mind if Jason comes along?" Brian asked.

"No problem," Frank said. "Lead the way."

As the Hardys drove their rented car behind Brian's Porsche and Jason's motorcycle, Joe asked, "How about some music?" He went to turn on the radio, when Frank suddenly remembered the tape he'd found in Marcus's trailer.

"Look what I found!" he said, reaching into his

pocket. "I think we should check this out," he told Joe, handing him the tape.

"Songs by Jason," Joe said, reading the label. He popped the tape into the cassette player. Jason's voice came blasting through the speakers, singing a song called "Can't Kiss Me." The tempo was slower and the words were different, but the chorus sounded remarkably like the Funky Four's latest single, "Can't Catch Me."

"There's something weird about this music," Joe said, straining to listen. "The vocals don't sound as if they were recorded at the same time as the rest of the tape."

"That doesn't seem unusual," Frank said, taking a turn, and keeping his eyes on Brian and Jason ahead of him. "Aren't most songs recorded in tracks?"

"Sure," Joe said. "And tracks are laid down one by one. But that's not what I mean. The music sounds like a professional recording, but the vocals sound as if they were put on later."

Frank listened and heard what Joe was talking about. The vocal track sounded muffled. "I know what you mean. The vocals were recorded with much lower sound quality."

"And unprofessionally," Joe said. "Oh well." He popped the tape out. "Maybe Jason had to finish the demo in a hurry. Anyway, he said it was an old tape. Maybe he didn't know too much about recording then. He probably figured it would still be okay to give it to Marcus like this."

"And Marcus must have rewritten it into 'Can't Catch Me.' At least that's how it sounds."

The Hardys followed Brian and Jason through heavy L.A. traffic. Soon they were driving along tree-lined streets, and all the cars around them were shiny and expensive. Finally, they pulled into the parking lot of a private Beverly Hills health club called Body Works. Brian and Jason led the Hardys into a vast weight room, equipped with all the latest and most elaborate fitness equipment.

Frank looked around with amazement. The room was filled with celebrities. A famous movie star was using the Stairmaster, a beautiful pop singer was on the stationary bicycle, and a TV talk show host was pumping iron.

Brian noticed Frank staring. "This club specializes in celebrities," he said with a smile. "I used to go to the YMCA but I got mobbed, so Marcus bought me a membership here."

Joe took a seat at a nearby weight machine and began to work his triceps. Frank chose a rowing machine and started pumping.

Brian started lifting two twenty-pound barbells. "Sometimes I think if I didn't work up a sweat at the gym everyday, I would go off the deep end."

"Especially lately," Jason remarked with a concerned frown. "You've really been under a lot of pressure. I'm worried about you, man."

"I'll be okay," Brian said with a sigh. "Still, sometimes I wish I could just blow off this whole rock star trip and take a vacation."

"I hear you," Jason said. "A month in the sun would feel good right about now."

"But it's just a dream. We have to finish our video and start promoting the single."

"Whatever you say, Brian," Jason said, wiping beads of sweat off his brow. "But your peace of mind means a lot more to me than any stupid single. Just remember that, buddy."

Jason finished ten reps on the weight machine and reached into his sweats for a small plastic bottle. He poured some scented lotion from the bottle onto his chest and rubbed it into his skin. "Here, try some of this," he told Frank and Joe. "I notice you guys got sunburns at the beach. This stuff will stop you from peeling."

Joe took the bottle and sniffed it. "Weird. What is it?"

Jason smiled. "A unique blend. That's patchouli you smell. Kind of funky, huh?"

"Yeah," Joe agreed, gingerly shaking a few drops onto his skin.

"That little worm!" Brian suddenly exclaimed.

Joe turned to see Pico Hernandez sauntering into the training room, dressed in skintight red workout clothes. Brian immediately jumped to his feet and ran over to confront him.

"You parasite!" Brian cried, ignoring the surprised stares of his fellow celebrities. "Get out of here. And leave me alone already!"

"Are you talking to me?" Pico asked, smiling.

"You know darn well I am," Brian shouted. "Why can't you give me any privacy? And what was that trick you pulled, putting all those articles in my trailer?"

"Lighten up, Brian," Pico said. "You're a celebrity, and that means you're fair game. If you don't want publicity, why don't you quit the band and go back where you came from?"

"Leave me alone!" Brian screamed furiously. "Or I'll find a way to sue you for all you're worth!"

Suddenly Pico stiffened and his eyes seemed to catch fire. "You think you're going to sue me? You little rat!" he yelled. Then he reared back and slugged Brian in the jaw.

10 Kidnapped!

Brian reeled backward and hit the floor. Instantly Pico was on top of him, throwing punches. Brian blocked the punches and threw one of his own, a solid right that connected with Pico's cheek.

Frank leapt into action. He threw himself on top of them. "Break it up!" he ordered, grabbing Pico around the chest and dragging him off Brian.

Brian immediately scrambled to his feet and made a lunge toward Pico, but Joe and Jason stepped in. They caught him by the arms and held him back. "Cool it, Bri," Jason said, squeezing his friend's shoulder.

A second later a security guard burst through the door and stepped between Brian and Pico. "Outside, both of you," he said. "And don't come back until you've calmed down."

Brian kicked the wall in frustration and strode out of the room. Pico tore himself from Frank's grasp and followed, a look of haughty pride in his dark eyes.

"I meant what I said in there," Brian muttered darkly, as they all stood in the parking lot and watched Pico drive away in his black Ferrari. "I don't have to sit back and let him get away with invading my privacy."

"I'm behind you all the way," Jason said, patting Brian on the back. He climbed onto his motorcycle. "You look stressed, man. I think you ought to go home and chill."

"Right," Brian said softly, gazing into the sky with a distracted expression in his striking green eyes. "I'm out of here." With barely a nod to the Hardys, he climbed into his Porsche and drove off.

Jason started up his bike and then looked back at Frank and Joe. "We're reshooting the performance footage at the Rialto tomorrow morning at eleven. See you there?"

"You bet," Frank said as Jason drove away. Then he turned to Joe. "Does it make sense that Pico would go so far as to hurt Brian just to get a story?" he asked. "I'm still not convinced."

Joe ran his hands through his hair. "Pico makes money writing about stars like Brian. It's not in his best interest to seriously hurt him—which is what could have happened on the Jet Ski."

Since it was late, Frank and Joe decided to return to their hotel room. Frank put in a call to the security at Magic World to see if they'd had any leads on who might have knocked out the operator at the ride the day before. He also contacted the hospital in Ositos and left a message for Dr. Fisher.

"I feel that there are a thousand loose ends in this case right now," Frank said with sigh. He leaned back on his bed and stared at the ceiling.

"That's because there are," Joe put in. "But tomorrow, let's check out Pico's offices."

"And look for what?" Frank asked, exasperated. "We don't have any solid leads as far as he's concerned."

Joe yawned and stretched. "We need to find out if Pico's the kind of person who would want to hurt Brian. Who else can tell us that but the people who work for him?"

"True enough," Frank agreed. "Come on, let's grab a bite to eat."

Frank and Joe ate dinner in the hotel restaurant and, after watching a movie on TV, fell asleep early.

The next morning, after a quick breakfast, Frank and Joe left the hotel early. Frank had looked up the address of *Dance Party Scene* in the phone book, and after a short drive, they pulled up in front of a three-story Spanish-style office building on Sunset Strip. Joe read the directory in the lobby. "Pico Hernandez, publisher. Third floor."

When they got to the third floor, Frank noticed two workmen carrying computer equipment out of the *Dance Party Scene* offices. Inside, a young woman with short dark hair and dressed in a black miniskirt and a Funky Four T-shirt was sitting at a desk, talking on the phone. A desk nameplate said her name was Hannah. "Can I help you?" she asked as she hung up.

"Uh, we want to apply for jobs as reporters," Joe said.

Frank shot him a look but went along with the ruse. "We know a lot about the music scene."

"You can fill out an application," Hannah said, leaning back in her chair and sizing up Frank and Joe. "But I'll tell you right now there are no openings."

"Well, maybe in a few months," Frank suggested.

Hannah shook her head sadly. "You guys look cool. Just between you and me, there aren't going to be any openings. The magazine is practically bankrupt. Defunct. Kablooey. Even I won't have a job after this week. Unless Pico gets his act together, and fast!"

"Bankrupt?" Joe said with surprise. "But *Dance Party Scene* is one of the best-selling music magazines in the country."

"It doesn't matter if you sell magazines, if you spend all your money on expensive cars." Hannah rolled her eyes. "The guy's a snake. I'm almost glad he's going under."

"Thanks for the information," Frank said, heading for the door. "You've been a big help."

"Try *Music Machine Monthly* over on Hollywood Boulevard," Hannah called out. "I hear they're looking for an editorial assistant."

Frank and Joe stepped into the hall and pushed the button for the elevator. "So now we know that besides being a sleaze, Pico is also a bad businessman," Frank said. "We're still no closer to knowing if he would actually try killing Brian. This case is driving me crazy."

Half an hour later, Frank and Joe arrived at the Rialto theater, where the Funky Four were shooting that day. Inside, the theater was swarming with reporters and photographers. The press seemed to be everywhere—snapping photos of the backup band as they set up, interviewing Lenny Wiseman, even chatting with the extras.

Brian was nowhere in sight, so Frank and Joe went to his dressing room. They found the door open and J.T. Eckert and Terry Solinsky inside.

"Hi, guys," Joe said. "What's with all the reporters?"

"Hi, Joe. Hi, Frank," Terry replied, leaning his lanky body against the wall. "It looks like the second *Dance Party Scene* hit the newsstands. Marcus's phone started ringing off the hook."

"What's in it?" Joe asked.

J.T. handed him a copy. Frank read it over Joe's shoulder. There was a front page story about how Brian had slugged Pico and even threatened him with a lawsuit.

"Everyone wants to know if Pico's article is true," Terry said. "So Marcus decided to open the set to the press to counteract the bad publicity."

"Where's Brian?" Frank asked, sitting on the edge of the dressing table.

"That's what we're wondering," J.T. said. "He was supposed to be here fifteen minutes ago. Marcus is planning a press conference to let Brian refute Pico's claims."

Frank realized now was the perfect time to question J.T. and Terry without Jason and Brian around. "What did you guys think of the article?" he asked, grabbing a chair and sitting on it backward.

"Totally lame," J.T. said, scrunching his boyish face into a look of disdain. "Brian's ego is no bigger than any other rock star's. If he sometimes gets a little testy, it's because he's under a lot of pressure. Pico probably deserved to get punched anyway."

"What about you guys?" Joe asked. "You seem to handle the demands of stardom pretty well."

At that moment, Mindy Beckett burst into the dressing room. "Brian," she said breathlessly, "Marcus is on the warpath. The press conference is starting and . . ." She stopped and gazed at the Hardys, J.T., and Terry. "Where's Brian?" she asked.

"He's not here," J.T. said. "Should we be worried?"

Mindy let out a harried sigh. "I'll look for him. You'd better go out front. Marcus and Jason are waiting for you."

Frank and Joe followed J.T. and Terry down the hall and out to the stage. Marcus and Lenny Wiseman were huddled in the wings, talking in anxious whispers. Jason was with them, looking a little worried himself. The first five rows of the theater were filled with reporters and photographers. The rest of the theater was taken up with extras for the video shoot. Frank spotted Pico Hernandez in the front row.

"There you are," Marcus said impatiently. Then, doing a double-take, he cried, "Where the heck is Brian?"

At that moment, a door at the back of the theater flew open and a uniformed messenger appeared. "Express letter for Marcus Malone," he announced.

"Up here," Marcus called.

The messenger jogged to the stage and handed over the letter. Marcus ripped it open. As he read it, his face went white and his mouth dropped open.

"What is it?" Frank asked anxiously.

"Brian's been kidnapped," Marcus said in a trembling voice. "If I don't hand over one million dollars ransom, he's going to die."

11 Taking the Hit

The reporters immediately jumped to their feet and began shouting out questions. "Read the letter!" a journalist cried, her notebook poised.

"Any idea who might be responsible, Mr. Malone?" another one asked.

"Are you going to contact the police?" Pico Hernandez shouted above everyone. He picked up his camera and took a close-up shot of Marcus's stunned expression.

The reporters were swarming the stage, and Marcus was looking overwhelmed. Frank turned to Joe and said, "Let's get these guys under control."

After leading the way up to the stage, Frank and Joe stood in front of the reporters, urging them back.

"Please, everybody sit down," Joe called out. "You'll get your answers, but you have to be patient."

While Joe dealt with the reporters, Frank approached Marcus, who still look shocked. He held the letter in his hand.

"Can I see that?" Frank asked gently. Marcus quickly handed over the letter. Frank saw that the message consisted of individual letters cut out from newspapers and magazines and glued to a plain white piece of paper. "I have Brian," Frank read. " 'I want one million dollars for his safe return. If you don't pay, Brian will die.' "

Jason, J.T., and Terry stepped up to read the letter over Frank's shoulder. "Poor Brian," Jason said.

"I wonder where he's being held captive," Terry added.

Suddenly Frank noticed that Pico Hernandez was packing up his camera and making a beeline for the door.

"Joe!" Frank cried. "Pico's about to bolt. Let's follow him."

Frank sprang off the stage and ran out the door that Pico had taken. He spotted the reporter about half a block up the street, getting into his black Ferrari. Frank turned and sprinted down the alley that led to the back of the Rialto. Joe was right on his heels. The two of them jumped into the rental car and backed out onto the street.

"There he is!" Joe cried.

Pico's Ferrari was heading up the hill to the intersection. The light turned red, and Frank pulled over behind a parked car a block away from the intersection so Pico wouldn't see him. "Why would he leave in the middle of such a big story?" Joe asked his brother. "He could lead us to an important clue."

"Good question," Frank said. Then, to his dismay, a policeman walked up to the car and tapped on the window. Frank rolled down the window. "You're in a no parking zone," the cop said. "I'll give you ten seconds to move—or would you rather I wrote out a ticket?"

"No, sir," Frank said. "Thank you, sir." He threw the car into drive and pulled forward to the light where Pico was waiting.

Slouching down in their seats, the Hardys furtively watched as Pico lit a cigarette and checked his reflection in the Ferrari's rearview mirror.

Glancing over at Pico's car, Frank's heart sank. Pico was looking right at him! The gossip columnist met Frank's eye and waved.

Pico lowered his passenger side window. "I saw you run out of the Rialto," he called. "Why are you following me?"

"We were wondering why you didn't stick around with the other reporters to question Marcus," Frank called back. "Maybe you already know where Brian is?"

98

"That's for me to know and you to find out," Pico said, revving the Ferrari's engine. "But in that heap of scrap metal, I doubt you will." With that, Pico hit the gas and took off, leaving a patch of rubber in the road. Within seconds, he was out of sight.

Frank slammed his fist against the steering wheel. "In our van we'd have had a chance at catching Pico. But in this rental car, no way."

"That weasel," Joe said. "He's long gone. Come on, let's get back to the Rialto. We need to get started on trying to figure out what happened with Brian."

Within ten minutes, the Hardys were back at the Rialto. Once inside, Frank saw that Marcus had regained his composure. "I plan to do whatever it takes to get Brian back unharmed," he was telling the reporters. "But I can also promise you this— Brian's kidnapper will eventually be apprehended, and when he is, I'm going to see to it that he goes to jail for a long, long time."

While the reporters continued to grill Marcus, Jason motioned Frank and Joe backstage. "I thought you guys were helping to guard Brian! Why aren't you doing something to find him?" he demanded.

"Until the kidnapper gives us more information, there's not much we can do," Frank replied.

With a weary expression on his face, Marcus joined the boys. "The reporters are finally leaving," the manager said. "I'm calling it a day. There's nothing we can do until the police hear from the kidnapper again."

"You've notified the police?" Joe asked.

Marcus nodded. "The only person who doesn't know yet about Brian is his mom."

Jason's eyes went wide. "Mrs. Bettencourt. Man, how are we going to tell her?"

Marcus rubbed his eyes and sighed. "The police have tried calling her, but her phone doesn't seem to be working. I suggested someone go out there and tell her personally. It's going to be quite a shock."

"I could go," Jason offered.

"Sorry, Jase. No way." Marcus held up his palm. "We don't know if it's safe for you to go anywhere. What if the kidnapper goes after you next? The police want me to rent a hotel room for you guys and keep you there."

"But if Mrs. Bettencourt hears about this from a stranger or on the news—" Jason said.

"We'll go," Frank offered.

"We will?" Joe asked.

"Sure," Frank said. "It's not that we know her that well, but it's better than having some police officers show up at her door."

"Thanks, guys," Jason said earnestly. "Brian would appreciate it."

Marcus looked skeptical, but he agreed it would be best if Frank and Joe went out to Ositos. While Marcus gave the Hardys directions to Brian's mother's, Jason excused himself, thanking Frank and Joe before he left.

"I'm just going home to pick up a few things," Jason said to Marcus. "But call me there to let me know where we're all going to stay."

After Marcus had given the Hardys the phone number of the police officer in Los Angeles who was handling the kidnapping, the boys left the theater.

"I want to give this guy a call before we leave," Frank said, getting into the rental. "Let's head back to the hotel, pack some things, and I'll call before we leave for Ositos."

Three hours later, night was falling, and Frank was driving on a narrow winding road that led into the hills outside Ositos. Joe sat beside him, fooling with the radio. They'd spoken to the police officer before leaving L.A., but as Frank suspected, there wasn't any news. The kidnapper had only sent the one note to Marcus, and so far he hadn't made any specific ransom demands.

"Are you sure this is the way?" Frank asked. The edge of the road seemed to drop off into nothingness, and he realized they were driving beside a steep cliff.

"Marcus said to take Route Forty-one west of Ositos," Joe replied, pausing on a dance music station that was playing a Funky Four song. "According to him, the house is just a couple more miles down the road.

101

"Hey, watch out!" Joe cried suddenly.

Frank glanced up to see a deer bounding across the road about fifty feet ahead. He slammed on the brakes. To his horror, nothing happened. Frantically, he tried the brakes again. Still nothing.

The deer was right in front of them. In another moment, the Hardys' car would broadside it. "Hold on," Frank shouted to his brother. "We're going to crash!"

12 Some Quick Steps

"Do something!" Joe cried, fear spreading across his face.

Frank assessed the situation in a split second. If he turned right, the car would plunge down the cliff. The only option was to turn left. Glancing over, he saw that the road was lined with tall pine trees. That meant he would have to immediately straighten out, all the while hoping he didn't meet a car coming in the opposite direction.

The deer was so close Frank could see its wide, frightened eyes. He spun the steering wheel hard to the left. The car veered across the double yellow line, missing the animal by inches, and barreled toward a pine tree.

"Watch out!" Joe yelled.

Quickly, Frank jerked up on the emergency brake and whipped the wheel back to the right as the deer disappeared into the bushes. The smell of burning rubber filled the air as the car screeched to a halt. When the dust cleared, Frank and Joe found themselves back in the right-hand lane, facing in the opposite direction.

"Nice driving," Joe said breathlessly. "A few more feet and we would been wrapped around a tree."

"Let's get the car off the road before someone comes along and slams into us," Frank replied, his heart pounding.

The brothers pushed the rental car to the other side of the road and let it roll to a halt between two pine trees. "What do you think happened?" Joe asked, leaning against the rear fender.

"The brakes worked fine all day today," Frank replied. He reached in his jeans and pulled out a pocket flashlight. "Let's check it out."

Joe opened the hood and together the brothers inspected the brake lines. Beneath the brake fluid reservoir, the main line was covered with thick brown fluid. Frank held the flashlight closer. "Look at that!" he exclaimed, pointing to a dozen small holes in the line. Brake fluid was oozing from each of them.

"Someone must have purposely punctured the

brake line," Joe said, "knowing the fluid would leak out and eventually cause the brakes to fail."

Frank straightened up and stared into the darkening sky. "But who?"

"Someone who knew where our car was, and who felt we were getting a little too nosy," Joe said, joining his brother at the edge of the road.

"What about Pico?" Frank suggested. "He knew we were following him. Maybe he turned the tables and followed us back to the motel."

"It could have happened at the Rialto," Joe pointed out.

Frank thrust his cold hands into his pockets. The mountain air was chilly. "We're not going to get any closer to the truth standing out here in the middle of nowhere," he said. "It's only a couple of miles to Mrs. Bettencourt's house, right?"

Joe nodded. "I think so." He went back to the car to get a map, using Frank's flashlight to search for their location. "Here we are," he said, pointing to a spot on the map. "We should be there in half an hour—provided we don't fall down the cliff, get run over, or meet up with a bear."

Frank laughed. "Sounds like fun. Let's go."

After hiking along the road for several miles, Frank and Joe reached the two-story wooden house with a wraparound porch. The lights were on in the living room, and Frank could see crowded bookshelves and comfortable chairs.

The brothers stepped up to the front door and rang the bell. A moment later the door opened. When Joe saw who was standing there, his mouth fell open.

"Brian!" Frank gasped.

"Frank! Joe!" Brian exclaimed. He was dressed in old jeans and an Ositos Valley High School sweatshirt, and he looked happier and healthier than Joe had ever seen him. "What are you doing here?"

Frank narrowed his eyes in confusion. "Us? We should ask you the same question. Did the kidnapper let you go?"

"Kidnapper?" Brian said, his mouth dropping open in surprise. "What kidnapper?"

"What's going on?" Mrs. Bettencourt asked, stepping up behind Brian. Wearing slacks and a sweater, her blond hair pulled back into a ponytail, she looked completely recovered from her car accident. "Is something wrong?"

"Marcus got a kidnapping note," Joe said. "We came out here to tell your mother the news. About how you were abducted . . ."

"Which is obviously not the case," Frank finished.

"Kidnapping note?" Brian said blankly. "Look, I don't know what you're talking about. I needed to get away, so I left a note for Marcus telling him I was leaving town for a couple of days."

"You mean Marcus knows where you are?" Frank asked incredulously.

"Not exactly," Brian admitted. "I didn't tell him where I'd be. I knew if I did, he would fly out here and try to drag me back."

"Where did you leave the note?" Joe asked.

"On Marcus's desk in his Beverly Hills office," Brian said. "Look, why are you cross-examining me? I didn't do anything wrong."

"And you honestly don't know anything about a kidnapping note?" Frank asked.

"No," Brian insisted. "Now will you please tell me how you knew I was here?"

Frank let out a long sigh. "We didn't. We offered to come out here to tell your mother. Marcus couldn't get through on the phone and didn't want her to hear it on the news or from the police."

Mrs. Bettencourt laughed. "I rarely watch television," she said. "And my phone's been broken for two days. It just got fixed about half an hour ago."

Fifteen minutes later, the Hardys were sitting in front of the fireplace, sipping hot chocolate and eating homemade apple pie with Brian and his mother. Frank and Joe had filled Brian in on everything that had happened since he left Los Angeles, including their near disaster on the cliff road.

"It was bad enough when I knew some lunatic was out to get me," Brian said angrily, "but now he's after my friends, too." He stared into the fire. "Man, I just wish we could nail this dude."

"We will," Frank said, sounding more confident

than he felt. "But first we have to deal with your phony kidnapper."

"Do you think he's the same person who threw the liquid nitrogen on Brian in the hospital?" Mrs. Bettencourt asked, obviously concerned.

"Possibly," Joe replied, "although the two crimes seem very different." He turned to Brian. "Tell us more about the note you left Marcus."

"There's not much to tell," Brian said. "After that encounter at Body Works with Pico, I felt that I was about ready to go over the edge. All I could think about was getting away from the music world and coming home. So that afternoon I went to Marcus's office. He wasn't there, but his secretary said she'd leave my note on his desk. I guess somehow it must have gotten misplaced."

"Either that, or someone purposely took it and cooked up the phony kidnapping scheme," Frank suggested.

"Pretty clever," Joe mused. "Nobody knew where Brian was, and the phony kidnapper was pretty sure Brian wasn't going to tell anyone. All the culprit had to do was convince Marcus to pay the ransom money in the next two days. By the time you returned, he and the money would be long gone."

"Speaking of Marcus, I'd better call him and tell him I'm okay," Brian said. He stood up and walked into the kitchen.

Mrs. Bettencourt threw another log on the fire.

"How are you feeling after your accident?" Frank asked.

Before Mrs. Bettencourt could answer, Brian threw open the kitchen door and announced, "The kidnapper sent Marcus another note. He wants the money delivered to Point Zero in northern Malibu at six o'clock tomorrow morning."

"All right!" Joe exclaimed. "This is our chance to nail him."

"If we can get the police to back off," Frank said. "Otherwise there will be such a commotion, the kidnapper probably won't even stick around to collect the money. Brian," he called, "let me talk to Marcus."

Frank hurried into the kitchen with Joe right behind him. Brian handed over the phone. Frank quickly explained that he and Joe were private investigators. "We think we can catch the person behind this phony kidnapping scheme, but to do it, you need to call the police and tell them Brian's been found. And whatever you do, don't tell them about the second kidnapping note."

"What!" Marcus exclaimed. "You'll have to explain that one. Why should I lie to the police?"

"It's not lying. We really have found Brian," Frank pointed out. "But we need to nail that kidnapper by ourselves, and quietly."

It took a lot of explaining and convincing from Frank, but eventually Marcus agreed. "But if you don't catch the person who wrote those letters and get Brian back here by the day after tomorrow to shoot the rest of the video—"

"I know, I know," Frank said. "We're dead meat!"

"Something like that," Marcus said. "You take care of Brian now, you hear? That kid's important to me."

"We'll do our best," Frank said. He hung up and turned to Brian. "Pushy, isn't he?"

Brian laughed. "No kidding!" Then he added mysteriously, "But starting today, I just don't care anymore."

Joe awoke to the sound of an acoustic guitar being strummed somewhere in the distance. He checked the bedside clock in the Bettencourt's guest room. It was three A.M., but Joe felt like he'd just gotten to sleep. Last night Brian had called a towing service to arrange for the Hardys' rental car to be picked up. Finally they had gone to bed to catch a few hours sleep before their return to L.A. With a yawn, he leaned over to the next bed and shook his brother.

The Hardys pulled on their clothes and went downstairs. They found Brian sitting out on the front porch in the dark, strumming a guitar and singing a song about freedom. Joe was impressed. The song was much more melodic and sophisticated than most Funky Four tunes. "I never heard that one before," he said. "Is it on your new album?"

Brian shook his head. "I wrote it myself. I played it for Marcus, but he said it's all wrong for the Funky Four." Instead of frowning the way Brian usually did when he mentioned Marcus's controlling ways, he smiled. "But that's not going to bother me anymore," he said quietly.

"Why not?" Frank asked.

Brian just grinned and began strumming again. As Brian started to sing, Joe noticed an odd whirring sound in the distance. He stared into the darkness and saw a car parked among the trees at the edge of the Bettencourt front yard. Someone was sitting in the car, snapping photos. Joe stood up and stepped off the porch. The car was a Ferrari.

"Pico's here!" Joe exclaimed, running toward the car. Frank and Brian leapt up and followed. Sure enough, Pico Hernandez was sitting in his car, holding a camera with a telephoto lens. A flash momentarily blinded Joe.

"How did you know Brian was here?" Joe demanded.

As usual, Pico's smile was closer to a sneer. "And good morning to you, too," he replied.

"Just answer the question," Brian snapped.

"I didn't know," Pico answered. "I drove here to wrangle an interview about the kidnapping with Brian's mother. Imagine my surprise when I saw Mr. Rock Star himself sitting on the porch!"

While Pico was talking, Joe glanced into the back of the Ferrari and noticed a stack of *Dance Party Scene* magazines on the seat. "Hey, what's this?" He reached in the window and grabbed an issue from the top of the stack. Four letters had been cut from the cover—an A, two E's, and a P. He flipped through the magazine. A dozen other letters had been cut out.

"Don't touch that!" Pico cried. He got out of the car and tried to grab the magazine from Joe's hand.

"The letters on that cover look just like the ones that were on the ransom note," Frank said.

"And that means—" Joe began.

Brian finished the thought. "Pico sent the kidnap letter!" he cried.

13 A Sleazy Deal

"That's a lie!" Pico shouted. He yanked the magazine out of Joe's hand.

"Then what is that magazine doing in your car?" Frank demanded. "And why are the letters cut out like they were used to make a ransom note?"

"Explain that!" Brian added, stepping closer.

"I have no idea," Pico insisted. He got back in the Ferrari and revved the engine. "Now if you'll excuse me, I've got some important business to take care of." With that, he backed into the road and drove away.

"He's probably heading to Point Zero right now to collect his money," Frank said.

"He'd be stupid if he was," Joe said. "He saw

Brian just now, so he'd know that we know the kidnapping is a hoax."

Brian stared down the driveway where Pico had just disappeared. "There's only one way to find out," he said. "Let's get going."

Ten minutes later, the Hardys and Brian were cruising out to the highway in the green Range Rover Brian had driven to his mother's house.

"I've been thinking about the kidnapping note," Joe said, watching the mountains roll by from the backseat. Frank sat up front while Brian drove. "If Pico sent it, we'll find out soon enough. But who else could have written it?"

"I hate to suggest Marcus," Brian said, "but he could have found my letter, then thrown it away. Maybe he wrote the kidnapping note as a publicity stunt."

"You think Marcus would have the nerve to pull off a hoax like that?" Joe asked.

"Marcus will do whatever it takes to keep the Funky Four at the top of the pop charts," Brian answered. "And me under contract to him."

"It seems like a desperate act," Frank observed.

"Marcus Malone can be a desperate man," Brian said simply.

Two and a half hours later, Brian drove the Range Rover into the deserted Point Zero parking lot. The traffic had been light, and Brian made good time. According to the map, Joe saw they were in northern Malibu, just a few miles south of Ventura County.

Brian parked the car in the empty lot, about thirty feet above the beach. Joe stepped out and gazed over the edge of the lot, where a steep, rocky hillside sloped down to the ocean. Dawn was about to break and there was a pink glow in the sky just above the horizon.

"What time is it?" Joe asked, as Frank came over to where he was standing.

Frank checked his watch. "Twenty of six."

Brian rolled down his window. "Marcus said to go down to the water and look for a small cave in the side of the cliff," he explained. "You're supposed to leave the money in there. According to the letter, the kidnapper will release me exactly one hour later."

"You'd better stay here," Frank said to Brian. "Keep out of sight." He pointed to a dirt road that led from the parking lot to a spot just north of the cliffside. "Park over there. If the person who's behind this scheme sees you, he'll know we're wise to him."

"No problem," Brian replied. "I'll be invisible. But believe me, I sure will have my eyes and ears open! I'm not going to let this goon get away from us."

Joe opened the back of the car and pulled out a small suitcase. He and Frank had borrowed it from

115

Mrs. Bettencourt and filled it with stacks of paper to approximate the weight and feel of money. Joe knew that once the phony kidnapper opened the suitcase, he would realize it was a trick. But with any luck, Joe told himself, we'll have him in custody by then.

A narrow path started at the north side of the parking lot and led down the steep hillside to the beach. Joe led the way, carrying the suitcase, with Frank close behind. When they reached the sand, they paused and looked around. The tide was high and the ocean lapped gently against the shore, just a foot or two from the cliff. There was no one in sight.

Joe took out a pair of binoculars from his jacket pocket. He'd borrowed them from Brian, thinking they might need them to find the cave. He scanned the coastline with the binoculars, and finally located a rounded opening in the rocky hillside that was about three feet high and two feet wide.

"There's the cave," Joe said, his excitement rising. "How about this for a plan. I'll hide inside," he suggested. "When the phony kidnapper crawls in to look for the suitcase, I'll grab him."

Frank nodded in agreement. "I'll hide back here, along the beach. Just in case I need to go for help. Good luck!"

Joe smiled. "No problem. When the going gets tough, Joe gets going!" Joe rolled up the bottom of his jeans and sloshed through the surf to the cave. He crawled inside and placed the suitcase at the entrance. In the pale morning light, Joe couldn't see anything behind the suitcase except shadows.

"Are you okay?" Joe heard Frank call out. "I can't see you."

"I'm fine," Joe replied. "It's pitch black in here, but I can feel the walls. The entire cave is probably no larger than four feet square."

"I'm heading down the beach," Frank shouted. "Yell if you need me."

Frank walked south about twenty yards until he reached a large patch of scrubby bushes. He knelt behind them and waited, his eyes riveted to the path. I hope the kidnapper hasn't seen me or Joe, Frank thought, or Brian up above.

Ten minutes later, Frank spotted a dark figure in a baggy hooded black windbreaker and dark pants at the north end of the beach. The stranger looked around cautiously, then scurried to the cave. As he knelt at the entrance, Frank stood up and edged closer.

The stranger reached for the suitcase. Frank saw Joe's arms lunge forward and grab for the man's legs. But the suspect was too fast. Seeming to defy gravity, he grabbed the suitcase and leapt straight up into the air, landing just beyond Joe's grasp.

"Stop right where you are!" Frank shouted, breaking into a run. Ignoring him, the dark figure scrambled onto a rock and began climbing up the cliff. As he climbed, he dislodged chunks of rock, dirt, and sand, which then tumbled down the hillside. They landed at the entrance of the cave, partially covering it.

"Joe, get out!" Frank called, running up to help him.

With one arm protecting his head, Joe began crawling out of the cave. Large stones and sand fell around him. Joe coughed and stumbled. Frank grabbed Joe's shirt and began to pull him out, while simultaneously looking up at the would-be kidnapper. The man was halfway up the cliff and climbing fast.

Suddenly the stranger lost his grip on the suitcase. It tumbled down the hillside, sending even bigger hunks of rock plummeting toward the beach. Instinctively Frank leapt back and covered his head. To his horror, he saw the suitcase bounce off the side of the cliff and fall on Joe's head.

Joe groaned and fell to his stomach. Frank scrambled to his feet and rushed to his brother's side. "Joe," he cried, turning him over, "are you all right?"

There was a large gash on the top of Joe's head. Blood was dripping down his face. "Forget about me," he said, his eyelids fluttering. "Get the bad guy."

Frank hesitated. But when Joe gave him a shove,

Frank decided his brother was right. Jumping up, he turned and started running up the path toward the parking lot. As he ran, he saw the suspect reach the top of the cliff and struggle to his feet.

He's getting away! Frank thought with frustration. Panting hard, Frank reached the top of the path. There, Frank saw that Brian had climbed out of the Range Rover and was running toward the stranger.

"All right!" Frank cried in excitement. "Give it up!" he shouted at the hooded figure. "We've got you cornered!"

The stranger froze and glanced quickly from Brian to Frank and back again. The hood cast a shadow across his face, obscuring it. As Brian and Frank moved closer, the person suddenly turned and ran south along the edge of the cliff.

"Stop!" Frank warned, breaking into a run. Out of the corner of his eye, he saw Brian running, too. The rock star reached the culprit first. With a grunt, he tackled the hooded figure and threw him to the ground near the edge of the cliff.

Frank heard the sound of shoes slapping against blacktop. He looked over his shoulder and saw Joe running across the parking lot. "Over here!" Frank shouted.

At the edge of the cliff, Brian was making a valiant effort to pin the stranger to the ground. But the man threw a punch that connected with Brian's eye, sending him reeling backward. The stranger used the opportunity to roll away from Brian and scramble to his feet.

"Let's get him!" Frank cried. Together he and Joe ran to the edge of the cliff. Frank got there first and shoved the stranger with his shoulder, throwing him backward onto the ground. As he landed, he rolled back over the edge of the cliff.

For one terrible moment, time seemed to stand still. In slow motion, Frank threw his arms out in a desperate attempt to catch the stranger. Out of the corner of his eye, he saw Joe and Brian doing the same. But it was no use. The hooded stranger fell off the hillside, screaming and thrushing wildly in the air. He landed with a thud and a splash in the water.

For a second, everything was silent. Then a high-pitched voice split the stillness. "Help!" the voice cried. "I can't swim!"

Frank, Joe, and Brian looked at each other. "I know that voice," Frank said with amazement.

"So do I," Joe said. "It's—"

Brian finished the sentence for him. "Suzi B.!" he exclaimed.

14 One Mystery Solved

"Help!" Suzi B. screamed. "I'm drowning!"

Frank, Joe, and Brian ran down the path at top speed, tripping and stumbling in their haste to save Suzi. Joe reached the beach first and saw the choreographer thrashing madly in the water about ten feet offshore.

Joe threw himself into the surf and started to swim. It was only then that he realized Suzi was flailing about in waist-deep water. With a laugh, he stood up and walked over to her. "Stand up," he instructed.

"Help!" she wailed, frantically grabbing at his legs.

"Stand up, I said!" He reached down, slipped his

hands under her armpits, and hoisted her to her feet.

Suzi opened her mouth to scream again. Then suddenly she realized she was standing up with her face three feet above the water. "Oh!" she gasped.

"You okay?" Joe asked.

Instead of answering, Suzi shoved him hard with her palms and sent him toppling backward into the water. Turning, she took off running toward the cliff. As Joe sat up he saw Frank and Brian run after her. They caught up with her and grabbed her just as she began climbing again.

"Let me go!" Suzi screamed, struggling wildly.

"Not a chance," Frank said, tightening his grip on her arms.

"Are you all right?" Joe asked, joining them. "You could have killed yourself falling down that cliff."

"I'm sorry," Frank said. "I didn't mean for you to get hurt."

Suzi closed her eyes and put her hand to an ugly bump that was forming on her forehead. "Ouch," she said, touching her head. "My head is killing me. I must have bumped it when I fell." For the first time since they'd nabbed her, Suzi seemed to calm down a bit. She moved her arms and legs thoughtfully. "But I guess the sand and water cushioned my fall," she said. "I'm sure I'll be hurting tomorrow."

"Why did you do it, Suzi?" Brian asked. "Why did you pretend you kidnapped me?"

"Because you owe me!" Suzi said heatedly. "You had me fired. And you encouraged Marcus to steal my song."

Brian grabbed Suzi's shoulders between his hands and stared her straight in the eye. "Please believe me, Suzi," he said with quiet intensity. "I did not want you to be fired. And I absolutely did *not* give your tape to Marcus."

"Why should I believe you?" she demanded.

"Because we're friends. Or we were once, anyway."

Suzi paused, and her angry expression slowly crumbled. She sank down onto the sand, turned her head away, and burst into tears. "I'm sorry," she sobbed. "I know I've been acting crazy, but you've got to understand that choreographing for the Funky Four was my first big break. I was working as an aerobics instructor and dancing in clubs on the weekends. Then Marcus saw me dance and gave me a shot. In one month I went from a roach-infested studio apartment in Silver Lake to a big house in the Hollywood Hills. I was somebody. Then I got fired and it all disappeared."

"So you decided to get even," Frank said.

Suzi nodded. "Two nights ago I sneaked into Marcus's office to search for my cassette tape. That's when I saw the note Brian had left on the desk. The whole kidnapping scheme came to me in a flash. I wrote the ransom note by cutting letters out of *Dance Party Scene*. Then I went over to Pico's

123

offices and tossed the magazines into the backseat of his car."

Brian said, as he put his arm around Suzi, trying to calm her down, "Suzi, didn't it occur to you that kidnapping is a crime?"

"But I didn't really kidnap you, did I?" Suzi answered. "Anyway, what's a million bucks to Marcus Malone? He must make that much in one month."

"But what about the other incidents?" Frank asked. "The microphone that almost electrocuted Brian, the Raging Tunnel ride, and all the rest. Are you responsible for those, too?"

"No, I swear it," Suzi said adamantly, her tears drying now. Her mouth set into a grim expression. "I wouldn't know the first thing about wiring a microphone or anything like that. All I know about is dancing. And Rollerblading, of course."

Frank gazed into the woman's teary eyes and felt she was telling the truth.

"Speaking of music," Joe said. "I just thought of something. Remember that tape we found in Marcus's office?" Frank nodded, and Joe went on. "We listened to a tape Jason made, a demo for 'Can't Catch Me' called 'Can't Kiss Me.'"

"That's my song!" Suzi shouted. She got up from where she was sitting and rushed Joe. "Where is the tape?"

"In my duffel bag," Joe said. At Frank's surprised

look, Joe said, "I'm a pack rat, what can I say? When we cleared our stuff out of the rental car, I grabbed the tape."

"I want to hear it!" Suzi cried. "Now."

The four of them hiked back up the cliff to Brian's car. Joe got the tape out of his duffel bag and popped it in the car stereo. He cued it up to the song, and soon Jason's voice came on, singing the lyrics.

"That's my music, but those aren't my vocals," Suzi said, frowning at the tape. "Listen to that. Jason must have dubbed out my voice and put his on instead."

"Jason must have stolen this tape from Brian, and then recorded his vocals over Suzi's. Then he obviously passed the tape along to Marcus," Frank concluded.

Brian rubbed his face, letting the news sink in. "I can't believe Jason would do that. He stood by all those times, letting you accuse Marcus of stealing your song."

"And claiming it was his!" Suzi added. "But it was always my word against his."

"Maybe Marcus is the liar," Joe suggested.

"There's only one way to find out," Brian said forcefully, popping the tape from the cassette and leaning back in his seat. "And that's ask him—right to his face."

"Finally!" Suzi said, smiling triumphantly.

"Someone believes I'm really the person who wrote that song! Maybe this whole kidnapping scheme was worth it," she joked.

Brian checked his watch and let out a low whistle. "Shoot. I've got to get going. We're filming the skydiving scene, and I've got a nine o'clock call."

Suzi had started shivering in the cold. Even though the sun was up, it was still a chilly morning. "I better get going, too," she said. "That's my car over there." She pointed out a battered hatchback. "Umm," she said uncomfortably. "You're not going to call the police, are you?" Suzi asked in a small, pleading voice.

"We have to report what happened today," Frank answered. "It's up to Brian if he wants to press charges."

Brian looked at Suzi thoughtfully. "I won't—if you promise to leave me alone from now on."

"I promise," Suzi said firmly.

With that, Suzi took off for her car. Joe glanced out at the water. The sun was up and the sky was streaked with pink and blue. "Well, we've solved one mystery," he said.

"Two, actually," Frank replied. "Since Suzi can't swim, we know she wasn't the one who sabotaged the Jet Ski."

"Right, but who did? And who's responsible for all the other attempts on Brian's life?"

"I don't know," Frank said seriously. "But if we

126

don't solve this case soon, the next attempt might be the one that succeeds."

Two hours later, Brian pulled into the parking lot of the Orange County Airfield. The film crew was already there, setting up their equipment. Brian parked and quickly led the Hardys across the airfield to the video set. Frank, an avid airplane buff, looked around with interest. The airfield was small, with one runway, a control tower, and five hangars. A dozen or more Piper Cubs, Cessnas, and gliders were parked in and around the hangars.

Lenny Wiseman and the crew had set up their trailers and equipment outside hangar five. The set was crawling with reporters, including Pico Hernandez, whom Frank spotted snapping photos of Jason, J.T., and Terry.

"There they are," Mindy announced, walking up with Marcus Malone and Lenny Wiseman to meet Brian and the Hardys. "The heroes who found Brian and caught his would-be kidnapper." She patted them on the back. "Good going, guys!"

"It's great news," Marcus said, beaming and obviously relieved. He gave Brian a huge bear hug, then stood back and said, "But who would have thought it was Suzi B.?"

Before Frank or Joe could question Marcus about Suzi's tape, the manager was ushering his star toward a makeup trailer. "Let's get to work," he said. "Lenny wants to shoot some close-ups of you and the guys."

"What scene are you filming today?" Frank asked Lenny.

"In this section of the video," Lenny explained, "the Funky Four are skydiving when suddenly we see that Marcella and her henchmen are hiding in the cockpit. They jump out of the plane after the Funky Four and there's a midair knife fight between the bad guys and Brian."

"Would you like to be extras?" Mindy asked the Hardys. "You could be members of the ground crew."

"We can do better than that," Frank said. "Joe and I are both experienced skydivers. I can play one of the henchmen and Joe can double for Brian, just as we did on the Jet Skis."

"Thanks," Brian broke in, "but I know how to skydive, too, and this time I'm doing my own stunts."

"Absolutely out of the question!" Marcus roared.

Frank looked at Brian. Normally, the rock star squirmed under Marcus's orders like a racehorse under a tight saddle. But today Brian looked totally relaxed. "I'm going up in the plane," he said calmly, "and I'm doing the dive."

"Have you read your contract lately?" Marcus growled.

"Think again," Brian said quietly. "If you want to take me to court for disobeying you, go ahead.

But I'm through being treated like a brainless child. I'm skydiving and that's final."

"What's going on, Bri?" Frank looked up to see Jason walk up to join them.

"You know I'm a good skydiver," Brian said to his friend. "I've done almost twenty jumps, and I don't need a stunt double for this scene."

"It's true," Jason said to Marcus. "I've seen him in action."

"But what if something goes wrong?" Marcus asked, worried.

"Nothing will go wrong," Brian insisted.

"All right, all right," Marcus cried, throwing up his arms in frustration, "do the jump if you want, Brian. But you'd better nail the shot on the first take or I'll have your head. This video is over budget already."

Lenny and the crew spent the next hour filming shots of the Funky Four suiting up and boarding the plane. Then Lenny went over the details of the upcoming jump move by move until everyone knew what was expected of him. Finally, they were ready to film the actual jump. Brian was to be one of the skydivers, as were one stuntwoman and seven stuntmen, including Frank and Joe.

As Brian and the Hardys walked toward the twin-engine Cessna that was waiting to take the skydivers and the cameramen into the air, Jason and a crew member came jogging out of the hangar with an armload of parachutes. "Here," Jason said, handing Brian a main chute and an emergency chute. "Go for it, Brian."

"Thanks," Brian replied, strapping his main chute over his red and white jumpsuit and his emergency chute around his waist.

The rest of the parachutes were handed out, and Brian boarded the first plane with Frank, Joe, the stunt doubles, Lenny, and the camera crew. The pilot taxied to the runway and took off. As the Cessna lifted into the air, Frank looked out the window at the rest of the crew and the reporters watching from the ground. With each passing second, they got smaller and smaller until they seemed no larger than tiny ants. Off to the south, Frank made out the ocean, and the shoreline. White foam dappled the waves as they broke onto the beach.

The plane circled the airfield until it reached a spot in an open field where a second camera crew was ready to film the descent from the ground.

"Places everyone," Lenny called. "Remember, Brian and the three stuntmen who are impersonating the Funky Four jump first. Then, when I give the signal, the rest of you will jump."

Brian, the Hardys, and the other stuntmen strapped on their helmets and waited in the open door. "Ground crew and air crew, roll cameras!" Lenny shouted into his walkie-talkie.

"Rolling," said the cameraman in the plane.

"Rolling," said the ground crew through the walkie-talkie.

"Action!" Lenny cried.

Brian grinned from ear to ear and gave Frank and Joe the thumbs-up sign. Frank felt his heart pounding in his chest as he watched Joe get ready to jump.

"Let's do it!" Brian cried. And with that, the teen star let out a whoop and leapt out of the plane, followed closely by the Funky Four impersonators. Frank and Joe stood in the doorway, watching them sail through the air.

"Bad guys, jump!" Lenny shouted.

Frank leapt out into open space, his heart pounding with exhilaration. Below him, the ground was a swirling blur of color. Out of the corner of his eye, he saw Joe and the other stunt doubles jumping from the plane one by one. They sailed through the air, waiting to open their parachutes. Lenny had told them to fly below Brian, leaving him alone with Marcella and the bad guys.

Frank caught a wind current and sailed toward Brian. With perfect precision, he pulled a prop knife from his belt and pretended to attack the rock star. Brian responded by pretending to punch Frank in the nose. All around them, Joe and the rest of the stuntmen acted out their own midair fight.

When it was all over, Frank saw Brian give the thumbs-up sign and reach for his ripcord. He pulled . . . then pulled again. But the chute didn't open.

With a panicked look in his eyes, Brian reached down to his waist and pulled the pin to release his emergency parachute. But that chute didn't open either.

Frank watched in horror as Brian twisted and thrashed through the empty air, desperately trying to release his chutes with his hands.

But it was no use. Brian was falling fast, plummeting toward the ground like a deadweight!

15 Crash Landing

"Help!" Brian screamed. "I'm going to crash!"

Frank's heart skipped a beat as he looked below at Joe and the other stuntmen. They had opened their parachutes and were floating gently to earth, unaware of Brian's predicament. Frank knew at that moment if anyone was going to save Brian, it had to be him.

"Brian," Frank shouted. "I'm going to try to dive close to you! Grab hold of me when I go past!"

Brian stared up at him with wide, frightened eyes. Frank wasn't sure if the singer had understood him. Ignoring the panicked feeling that rose up in his chest, Frank moved his arms into a diving position, pressed his legs tightly together, and tilted his body forward. Immediately he began plunging downward, directly toward Brian's twisting body.

"Now!" Frank shouted, stretching out his arms. "Grab me!"

Brian reached out for Frank, but he wasn't fast enough. The strong winds sent Frank soaring, and Brian was left clutching at empty air.

Frank let out a groan of frustration, then stabilized himself and looked around. Brian was above him now, still falling through the sky with his arms outstretched and his mouth open in a silent scream. Down below, Joe and the others had become aware of what was happening and were looking on in helpless horror.

Frank glanced downward. The ground was moving toward him at sickening speed. Frank knew he had only one more chance. If he didn't catch Brian this time, he would have to release his chute to save himself and let Brian crash. But even if he succeeded, he wasn't home free. There was no guarantee Frank's chute would open in time, or that it would be strong enough to handle two people.

"I'm here, Brian!" he shouted, catching a wind current and stretching out his arms. "Grab hold!"

Brian flung out his arms as he plummeted past. Frank lunged forward and grabbed for them. For a moment, the wind held him back. The two teenagers hung there, their hands only inches apart. Then suddenly, Frank felt the sleeve of Brian's jumpsuit touch his hand. Frantically, he clutched at it.

"I've got you!" Frank cried. "Hold on!"

With all his strength, Frank pulled Brian toward him and caught the rock star in a viselike bear hug. Brian responded by flinging his arms around Frank's waist.

"I'm with you," Brian said. "Pull your chute. Quick!"

Frank wrenched his right arm free and pulled his ripcord. The force of the chute opening jerked them both upward, and the wind rushed by with a reassuring whoosh.

Frank looked down. The ground was still coming up fast. He and Brian had fallen so quickly they had passed Joe and the stuntmen, who just watched them fly by.

"Brace yourself," Frank urged.

The fall came a few seconds later. Together he and Brian hit the grass and rolled.

Then suddenly, it was over, and the two teenagers were lying motionless in the field with Frank's parachute billowing out behind them. "You saved my life," Brian said in a shaky voice.

But before Frank could answer, he and Brian were surrounded by a crowd of people, shouting and pulling them to their feet.

"Are you all right?" Mindy Beckett cried.

"I . . . I think so," Brian stammered.

"You are so stubborn!" Marcus roared. "I told you not to jump. You could have been killed!"

"How did it feel when your chute didn't open?"

Pico Hernandez asked, sticking a microphone in Brian's face.

"Get lost, Hernandez," Jason growled, shoving the reporter aside. Jason put his arm around Brian's shoulders. "Brian, buddy," he said anxiously, "I can't believe it! I watched the whole thing and I was sure you were a goner. Boy, am I glad you're okay."

While everyone was fussing over Brian, Frank stepped back and watched as Joe and the stuntmen landed. "Whew!" Frank exclaimed, jogging up to join his brother. "That was a close call."

"No kidding," Joe said. "It was killing me to watch you and not be able to do anything. But you can bet I'm going to do something now."

"What do you mean?" Frank asked.

Joe glanced around to be sure no one was listening. He lowered his voice and said, "Have you ever noticed how Jason is never around when these accidents happen to Brian?"

Frank thought it over and realized Joe was right. "It's true. Remember that day at the Santa Monica pier? He went to get something to eat just before the Jet Ski malfunctioned."

"And at the hospital in Ositos," Joe went on. "Jason split just a few minutes before the mysterious orderly threw liquid nitrogen on Brian."

"But why would Jason be behind all this?" Frank asked. "He and Brian are best friends."

"Maybe their friendship isn't all it's cracked up

to be," Joe said. He gathered up his parachute. "Come on, let's check this out."

Ten minutes later, Frank and Joe were inside a huge hangar, talking to the head of the flight crew, Bob Coursen, a tall man with shaggy brown hair and a drooping mustache.

"That's right," the man replied. "Nice kid. You'd never guess he was a big star."

"And do you think Jason could have tampered with the chutes?" Joe asked.

Coursen frowned. "He asked if he could help hand out the chutes to the stuntmen, but that doesn't prove he fooled around with them."

"Did he ask you any questions about how the parachutes were packed?" Frank wanted to know.

Bob nodded slowly and raised his bushy eyebrows. "Come to think of it, he did. He seemed real interested. Wanted to know if I'd ever seen a chute malfunction. You know how kids are. They like to hear about the gory stuff."

"And you told him?" Joe asked.

"Well, yes. I told him about a guy who was killed when his chute didn't open." Bob frowned slightly, and went on. "Turns out his cords were wrapped real tight around his chute. He had packed it himself. Didn't do the job right."

"Thanks, Mr. Coursen," Frank said. "You've been a big help."

"No problem." Mr. Coursen paused. "He

seemed like such a nice kid," he said, a note of uncertainty creeping into his voice.

The Hardys left the hangar and stepped out into the sun. Frank shook his head sadly. "I can't believe Jason tampered with Brian's parachute."

"It's a deadly stunt," Joe agreed. "But that's how it looks to me."

Frank agreed. "Me too. The only problem is, if we confront Jason, he's sure to deny it." He gazed pensively at the video crew trailers that were lined up outside the hangar and realized that they had a golden opportunity to investigate Jason—without him knowing.

"Come on," he said to his brother. "What Jason doesn't know won't hurt him."

Frank led the way to Jason's trailer and tried the door. The knob didn't turn. The Hardys glanced around to make sure no one was in sight, then Frank slammed his shoulder against it. The flimsy lock popped open. "Bingo," said Frank.

Joe stepped inside, followed by his older brother. "What are we looking for?" he asked.

"Anything that connects Jason to those accidents," Frank said, scanning the room. The trailer was immaculately clean and neat. Jason's clothes were hung carefully in the closet. A small refrigerator was filled with bottled water and fruit.

Joe started searching through the closet while Frank checked under the bed. The floor was littered with papers, tools, hardware, and a black gym bag.

Frank pulled out the bag and unzipped it. "Wow!" he gasped. "Check this out!"

Inside were a Jet Ski repair manual, a remote control device, and a pair of sunglasses.

"Those are the ones Brian was wearing the day we met him at the video arcade," Joe said, his eyes wide. "The ones Jason must have pulled off Brian's face."

Frank was about to answer when the sound of car engines broke the silence. With a start, Frank grabbed the gym bag. "Let's get out of here," he shouted.

He and Joe hurried outside. The Funky Four and the video crew were returning in the crew trucks. Frank hid the bag behind his back as Brian, Jason, J.T., and Terry got out of a vehicle.

"Hi, guys!" Brian called, walking up to join them.

"Hey, the door to my trailer is open!" Jason cried suddenly. He started toward it, but Frank blocked his way.

"Hang on," he said, producing the gym bag from behind his back. "Brian, I found a few things in Jason's trailer that might interest you."

"You went into my trailer?" Jason demanded. "That's breaking and entering, man. I could have you arrested!"

"The police are going to be much more interested

in arresting you than me when they see this," Joe said. He grabbed the bag from Frank and held it out for Brian to see. "We found the repair manual and the remote control Jason used to sabotage the Jet Ski. Plus, here are the sunglasses he ripped off you at the video arcade."

Brian's expression was one of shock and confusion. "You think Jason is responsible for the attempts on my life?" he asked with an incredulous laugh. "Get real! He's my best friend."

"Can we see the parachute you were wearing?" Frank asked calmly.

"Sure," Brian replied, pulling his main and back-up chutes out of the back of the truck and handing them to Frank. "But why?"

The older Hardy opened the nylon parachutes. His eyes went wide when he saw that the cords were wrapped tightly around the chutes.

"These chutes have been tampered with," Frank said, holding them up for Brian's inspection. "It would take an hour just to get the cords unwound."

"That clinches it," Joe said. "Jason's our mystery saboteur!"

16 A Different Tune

"Oh, come on, Bri," Jason said with a forced laugh. "You don't believe these guys, do you? They're just a couple of kids playing detective. They can't prove a thing."

Brian didn't answer. He looked from Jason to the Hardy brothers and back to Jason again. A jumble of emotions flickered across his face: disbelief, confusion, realization, pain. "Why?" he said at last.

Jason clenched his fists. A small muscle under his eye twitched involuntarily. It seemed to Joe he was trying desperately to keep his emotions under control. Then suddenly, Jason lunged forward and grabbed Brian by the front of his jumpsuit.

"Because . . . because you have what I want," he blurted out.

"What?" Brian gasped.

"Don't stand there looking so innocent," Jason shouted, his eyes flashing with fury. "You know what I mean. You're the big star, but I'm the one who started this group. To you it was just a hobby, but for me it was everything. It was my whole life." He let go of Brian's shirt and pushed him away. "I'm supposed to be the lead singer. I deserve to be the superstar, not you!"

As Jason's voice rose, a few crew members turned to listen. Soon more and more people began drifting over—reporters, photographers, J.T. and Terry, Marcus Malone, Lenny Wiseman, and Mindy Beckett.

"So you decided to get rid of Brian?" Joe said in disbelief.

"That's right," Jason answered. "As long as he was around, I knew Marcus would never let me be the lead singer. But with Brian out of the picture, Marcus would have to give me a chance."

"You mean you wanted to kill me?" Brian asked in disbelief.

"Jason," Marcus cried, "I can't believe what I'm hearing. Brian's your friend. You guys started out together."

"Big deal," Jason said, his dark eyes flashing. He shrugged. "I knew Brian was stressed out from working so hard. Marcus was getting on his nerves and our contract was up for renewal. I figured if I made it look like some mysterious enemy was out to get Brian, he might get fed up with show business and quit the group."

"So you arranged a few accidents," Frank said. "Like the spotlight that almost fell on Brian's head, and the microphone that short-circuited."

"That's right," Jason admitted. "But I positioned the light so it would fall in front of Brian, and the current on the mike was turned down."

"Did you program the computer at Magic World to make my car derail?" Brian asked incredulously.

Jason nodded. "I stole a hospital orderly's uniform and threw liquid nitrogen on you, too. I sabotaged the Jet Ski, too, figuring you'd be on it."

"What about Suzi B.'s tape?" Joe broke in. "You took it from Brian's house and recorded your voice over Suzi's, didn't you?"

Marcus answered for Jason. "He came to my office and played me a demo tape," he explained. "He said it was his." Marcus's eyes narrowed. "If I had thought he was really stealing Suzi's music, you can believe I wouldn't have used the song."

"I needed to remind you how valuable I am to the group," Jason snapped. "A hit song would make you notice me."

Frank turned back to Jason. "What else are you responsible for?"

"I'll tell you what worked best," Jason replied, a slight smile flickering across his lips. "It was sticking those gossip columns and that note on Brian's dressing room mirror. I had a feeling that would push him over the edge, and I was right. When we went to the health club and Brian attacked Pico, I knew he was thinking seriously about chucking everything and running away."

"It's true," Brian admitted. "When I left the note on Marcus's desk and took off for Ositos, I wasn't sure if I was ever coming back. But in the end, I did."

"That's when I knew you were never going to quit the group," Jason growled, his fists clenched by his side. "So I tampered with the brakes on Frank and Joe's car, too. I knew they would find out about me, and I wasn't about to let myself get caught, so I had to get rid of them."

"Jason, I can't believe what I'm hearing," Brian said sadly. "I thought our friendship meant more to you than gold records."

"Think again," Jason shot back. Then suddenly, his eyes filled with tears. "You've got the looks, the charm, the voice. You don't even have to try. It's just not fair!"

"So you decided to even the score by tampering with Brian's parachute," Joe said.

"I was fed up," Jason said desperately. "I lost my head."

"That's attempted murder," Frank pointed out. "You could go to jail for that."

Jason's eyes narrowed. He scanned the crowd, obviously looking for a way out. Joe realized at that moment that the reason Jason had been so willing to confess so much was because he'd been stalling for time. Joe primed himself for Jason's attempt at escaping, which he just knew would come.

"Not if I don't get caught," Jason said. With that, he turned and ran, shoving his way through the startled crowd that had gathered to listen.

"Stop him!" Joe shouted.

But it was too late. Jason had broken through the throng and was running toward his trailer. Frank, Joe, and Brian hurried after him, but he disappeared around the back and appeared a moment later on his motorcycle. "So long, dudes!" he shouted, roaring past them in the direction of the parking lot.

Joe knew immediately they'd never catch Jason in the rental car. "Where's your Range Rover?" he asked Brian.

"Follow me," Brian answered, leading the Hardys behind his trailer. The Range Rover was parked a few feet away. "You drive," he told Joe, handing over the keys. "You've probably had more experience with high-speed chases."

Joe jumped into the driver's seat and started the engine. Frank sat in the passenger seat and Brian got in back. With a squeal of tires, Joe took off around the trailers and across the blacktop. Up ahead, he could see Jason heading across the parking lot to the road.

"We're going to lose him," Frank warned. Joe stepped on the gas and picked up speed until Jason was only fifty yards ahead of them.

Jason glanced over his shoulder. When he saw the Range Rover gaining on him he changed course, veering left across the open fields to the airfield runway.

"Where's he going?" Brian asked.

"Beats me," Frank replied. "Maybe he thinks we won't follow him onto the runway."

"That's where he's wrong," Joe said, steering the Ranger Rover across the bumpy field.

Up ahead, Jason zoomed onto the runway. Joe followed, the gap between them once again narrowing. Then suddenly a low whine split the air. Joe glanced into the rearview mirror and was startled to see a small biplane coming in for a landing. The plane was a mere two hundred feet above them and descending fast.

"Watch out, Joe!" Brian warned, catching sight of the plane. But Joe had already jerked the steering wheel to the right and was heading into the field. He hit the brakes and skidded to a halt as the plane roared past them.

Up ahead, Jason was still riding his Harley, oblivious to the airplane coming in behind him. "Get out of the way!" Brian shouted, but his voice was drowned out by the whine of the biplane.

Just then, Jason glanced over his shoulder and saw the plane roaring toward him. His face froze in horror and he began to swerve wildly. At the same time, the biplane pulled up hard to avoid crashing into the motorcycle. The blast of wind from the propeller blades sent the cycle toppling to the ground.

As the cycle fell, Jason was thrown into the air. He landed on the blacktop and rolled, finally coming to a stop on his stomach at the edge of the runway.

"Come on!" Brian shouted, leaping out of the car. With Frank and Joe right behind him, he ran to Jason's side.

"Jase, are you all right?" Brian asked, reaching out to roll his friend over.

Suddenly, Jason flipped onto his back and sat up. In his hand was a knife. He lunged at Brian, but Joe threw himself on Jason and grabbed the wrist that held the knife. Jason responded by grabbing Joe's hair with his free hand and pulling with all his might.

Joe cried out in pain, and his grasp on Jason's wrist weakened. Jason pulled his arm free and was about to raise the knife. But before he could strike, Frank grabbed Jason from behind and pinned him to the ground with his knees. Then Brian wrenched the knife from his hand and threw it into the open field.

"It's over, Jason," Frank announced. "Give it up."

Jason didn't struggle. He crawled slowly to his feet and hung his head.

The sound of sirens broke the silence. Joe looked up to see three police cars barreling across the fields with their lights flashing.

"You know, Jason, it's weird," Brian said sadly. "I used to look up to you. You had drive and ambition and you seemed to handle the fame better than the rest of us. I mean, I really thought you had it all together."

"You were wrong," Jason said quietly. "You're the one who has it together. Now don't blow it like I did."

Brian nodded. In the sky above him, the biplane circled for another landing. Then the patrol cars pulled up beside the runway and the police took Jason away.

"You know, I'm really going to miss California," Joe said as he and Frank checked their luggage at the L.A. airport the next morning. Brian was with them, wearing a baseball cap, fake mustache, and dark glasses so he wouldn't be recognized.

"It's been a perfect vacation," Frank agreed. "Sun, surf, and plenty of mystery."

"These last few days haven't exactly been my idea of a vacation," Brian said with a laugh. "Still, it all turned out for the best. I mean, if Jason hadn't

148

made my life so miserable, I probably never would have gotten the nerve to go out on my own."

The day before, after the police had taken Jason away, Brian had called an impromptu press conference in front of hangar five to announce that he was quitting the Funky Four to start a solo career. He planned to find a new manager and record an album consisting of all original songs.

"How did J.T. and Terry take the news of your solo career, Brian?" Frank asked.

"They understood where I was coming from," he replied. "Plus, I asked them to sing backup on my album and on my next tour, so in a way we'll still be together."

"Any chance the tour will bring you to Bayport?" Joe asked.

"You bet," he replied. "And you can be sure there'll be two front row tickets reserved for you guys, complete with backstage passes."

"All right!" Joe exclaimed. "Thanks!"

"You know, I talked to Suzi B. last night," Brian said as they walked to the gate. "She's going to take Marcus to court for her share of the royalties on her song. I told her I'd testify on her behalf."

"After the way she badmouthed you, that's really generous," Joe said.

"I don't want to turn into a jealous, vengeful person like Jason did," Brian answered.

"Sounds as if you've definitely got your priorities straight," Frank remarked.

"I hope so. Wow!" Brian exclaimed suddenly. "Look at that."

Frank followed Brian's gaze. A woman was sitting in the waiting area reading the latest issue of *Personality Magazine*. The headline on the cover said EXCLUSIVE PHOTOS OF BRIAN BEAT, UP CLOSE AND PERSONAL. Below was a photograph of Brian, sitting on his mother's porch playing the guitar. At his side were Frank and Joe.

"Hey," the woman reading the magazine suddenly cried, pointing at Frank and Joe, "I recognize you! You're the guys on the cover of *Personality*." She jumped to her feet. "Can I have your autograph?"

Suddenly everyone in the airport terminal was staring at Frank and Joe. A few young women rushed forward and surrounded them.

"Are they rock stars or movie stars?" someone asked eagerly.

"I don't know, but they're really cute!" a teenage girl cried.

Brian stood to one side, clearly enjoying the fact that for once someone else was getting all the attention. "Well, now you know what it feels like to be famous," he called to Frank and Joe. "What do you think?"

"I think I want to quit the business before I've even started!" Frank called as he pushed through the throng of people to board the plane.

"We'll stick to solving mysteries," Joe called as he followed Frank. "It's a whole lot safer."

NANCY DREW® MYSTERY STORIES By Carolyn Keene